ROSES
ARE
DEAD,
MY
LOVE

by
Penny Clover Petersen

This is a work of fiction. Names, characters, places, and incidents either are the product of the author's imagination or are used fictitiously. Any resemblance to actual events or locales or persons, living or dead, is entirely coincidental.

ISBN: 978-1-940758-03-9
Cover design by InstinctiveDesign

Published by:
Intrigue Publishing
11505 Cherry Tree Crossing RD #148
Cheltenham, MD 20623-9998

ROSES
ARE
DEAD,
MY
LOVE

To my parents
Lionel and Regina Clover
who loved a good mystery and a good laugh
and
To Rachel Anne and Matthew
who make my life so bright

April 17, 1953
Griffith Stadium
Washington, DC

"Do you think he'll sign it, Dad?"

"You bet. We'll just wait here. He should be along soon. Have you got your card and a pen ready?"

"Yeah. I made sure the pen wasn't leaky, too."

"Good boy. I think it's going to be a great game."

The boy bounced up and down like it was Christmas Eve. Suddenly he looked up and there was his hero walking right toward him. His jaw dropped open and he couldn't think of a thing to say. The man was almost to the gate when the boy's father gave him a shove forward.

The boy squeaked, "Sir."

The man turned toward him and smiled. "You got somethin' for me to sign?"

"Yes, sir. I've got your card. And a pen." He handed them to the player who smiled and signed his name on the card.

"Sir, could you put the date on it, too? 'Cause it's my birthday today."

"Sure." He added the date and said, "Happy birthday, kid. Gotta go to work now. Enjoy the game."

"Thank you, sir, I will. Could you hit one out for me, sir?"

"I'll sure try." He smiled and walked into Griffith Stadium through the players' entrance.

The boy looked up at his dad and grinned, then shouted, "I got Mickey Mantle's autograph!"

A flash went off and a man with a camera who'd been standing near the gate said, "What's your name, kid? I just might put you in tomorrow's paper."

Chapter One

Rose Forrest had just taken her mail out of her box and was leaving the post office when a man standing at the counter shouted, "Your job is to make sure I get all the mail that's mine! I needed this letter yesterday. What kind of place are you running here?"

The old lady behind the counter replied, "In your ear, buddy. You got a complaint, talk to the Post Master General."

"You can be sure I will!" He grabbed his letters, shoved past Rose, and steamed out the door. Rose caught it just before it slammed into her and snapped, "Thanks a lot!"

She pushed the door open again, walked out and watched the slammer as he stomped across the street in a huff. She followed in the same direction, noticed something fall from his hand and called out, "Oh, you dropped something!"

He didn't turn around. She trotted after him and called again, "Yoo-hoo, you with the problem!"

He didn't even pause. He just straightened his back and walked on.

Rose wrinkled her brow and murmured, "Freaking idiot!"

She tried again, her voice dropping to her best Sly Stallone mumble. "Yo, Adrian. You want I should pick that up?"

She stopped her trot, bent down and retrieved the Express Mail envelope she had seen slip from the pile he was carrying. "Hey, this might be important. You never know. You might have won Power Ball."

She stood and waved it in the air and yelled, "Finders

2

keepers. Do you want this damned thing or not?"

The man finally stopped walking and looked around. He turned to Rose and said, "What in God's name are you yelling about? Are you speaking to me? I heard you calling someone named Adrian."

Finally seeing the envelope in her hand, he started walking toward her. "Is that mine? I haven't got time for games. I was already running late and that damned Nazi in the post office has made me even later!"

He was fortyish, tall and slim with well-cut graying hair and eyes the color of smoky quartz behind wire-rimmed glasses – kind of bookish and sexy.

"Too bad he had to open his mouth," thought Rose. "He's quite the studly muffin."

She looked deep into the muffin's eyes and said, "It was a *Rocky* reference."

"Excuse me?"

"Yo, Adrian. You know, Sylvester Stallone. *Rocky*."

He just looked at her blankly.

Rose shook her head and narrowed her eyes. "Oh, screw it, buddy. I've got things to do, too. You dropped something. Right there."

She tossed the envelope into a small puddle on the side of the road. "Have a nice day," she chirped and strode off before he could answer.

Rose crossed the little bridge that spanned abandoned railroad tracks and connected the halves of Old Towne and continued down Azalea Lane. She came to her beautiful Victorian house with the sign reading *Champagne Taste* centered above the porch. When she reached the door she glanced back to see the studly muffin watching her as he moved slowly down the street.

She walked into the shop, threw the mail on the counter and went into her office. She opened the small refrigerator, got out the iced tea she had made earlier that morning and poured herself a glass, then added sugar and lemon to it. She took a sip and walked slowly back into the shop. She stood looking out the window, frowning.

Her sister, Daisy, walked in through the sunroom door fanning herself and said, "It is really too hot for June."

Rose answered, "Hmmph."

"What's with you?"

"People. Men. Really, just one incredible jerk I ran into at the post office. He and Peggy were going at it about some letter he should've gotten yesterday."

"Who's Peggy?"

"The woman who works there. You know her. The old witch that's been there forever."

"Hmm. I never knew her name! Old Witch fits so nicely. She scares me."

"Me, too. Anyway, he really lit into her. Of course, she gave as good as she got, sweet old soul that she is. Then as I was leaving, he practically slammed the door in my face."

Rose picked up the mail and started sorting through it.

"Even so, since I'm an incredibly nice person, I tried to bring his attention to a letter he dropped as he was goose-stepping across the bridge. You'd have thought I was trying to sell him insurance." Rose slammed her glass down, spilling tea on the counter.

"Now see what he's made me do." She grabbed a dust cloth and wiped up the tea. "What a jackass! He was really unpleasant. And it's a damned shame because he is very good looking."

"Oh, yes? What does he look like?"

"Tall. Well taller than I am. Grayish hair, nice brown eyes. Glasses. Reminds me of a prof I had in college."

"Sounds like our new neighbor. The guy who bought the Book Renew. Did you play nice and give him the letter?"

"More or less. It got a tad wet."

Champagne Taste was located in Old Towne, the heart of the historic district of Bostwick, Maryland, a bedroom community just ten miles from the White House. Old Towne was a thriving village of antiques dealers and small boutiques housed in old homes and buildings, many dating back to the Victorian era.

The inheritance came at a time when Daisy and Rose both needed a change. They moved into the top two stories of the house and converted them into a cozy apartment.

The first floor became an upscale gift boutique. It was their dream come true and things were going well. The shop was making money. They were their own bosses. They liked their neighbors. And, best of all, they hadn't found a dead body in over six months.

Daisy started dusting the crystal display. She handed Rose a dry cloth and said, "Here, you can start on the pewter. How did his letter get wet?"

"It jumped out of my hand and landed in a puddle. What do we know about this guy? Anything?"

"Some, but I got it from Mary Newhart, so I don't know if it's true or not."

Mary Newhart owned Newhart's Antiques right across the street from Champagne Taste. She was a nice, nosy woman who could be relied on to tell all whether or not it was exactly true.

"She told me his name is Peter Fleming. He's forty-two, and a college professor. She thinks he's at George Washington University. Apparently, the book shop will be just a part-time thing. He's divorced, no kids, no pets. Lives in Washington, DC just off Dupont Circle, drives a '73 Mercedes, and goes to church on Christmas and Easter. Wears Ralph Lauren boxers."

"Does he?"

"How should I know? I made that part up. Even Mary would have a hard time bringing underwear into a conversation with a total stranger. But she did tell me that he paid cash for the Book Renew. That's interesting."

"A Mercedes coupe!"

"A convertible. The little 450 SL. Silver."

"Even better. I think I'd look really good in a vintage convertible."

"You said he's a major jerk."

"He's probably having a bad day. From the little I overheard, Peggy put his mail in someone else's box. I guess I'd be a little miffed, too. And, he has nice eyes."

"And a nice car."

Rose smiled and said, "Yes, indeed!"

Daisy looked at her watch and said, "Hurry up with the pewter. It's almost time to open. Oh, Mother called and said she'll be here at noon so we can all go to lunch. She wants to take the dogs with us."

"Why? Much as I love the little critters, Malcolm and Percy aren't really poster puppies for the well behaved dog," said Rose.

Their mother, Angela Forrest, had gotten Malcolm for the girls last fall. The little black fur ball was supposed to be a watch dog. But like his brother Percy, Angela's own little mutt, the family trait ran more to a fondness for humping everything in sight, than watching the house.

"Where is our little bundle of hormones, anyway?"

Daisy answered, "I sent him outside while I was cleaning. He was being a pain in the butt. I think he wanted to go to the post office with you."

Rose gasped. "Outside? It's too hot today. It's not even ten o'clock and it's already ninety-two degrees. Nobody should be out in this weather."

"He's fine. He's got a gallon of cold water and that igloo of his stays nice and cool. I opened the air vents and he seemed happy enough."

Rose walked to the sunroom door in the back of the shop.

"Well. I'm letting him in. I'll put him upstairs if he gets too naughty."

Rose went into the back garden and walked over to the doggie igloo nestled under an old, black walnut tree. Malcolm poked his nose out and looked at her.

"Being a good boy? You can come out if you want, you know." Malcolm wriggled out and stretched his front paws. Rose scratched his head and gave him a treat.

"Grandmother is bringing Percy over to play in a little while. You can come into the shop if you get too hot. Okay?"

Malcolm just looked at her and did a little doggy nod, then wriggled back into the igloo.

Rose said, "I know. It's too damned hot for anything, even good-natured humping." She was walking back to the sunroom when a pretty orange tabby cat came out the pet door at the far end of the porch.

"Go back inside, you nut. It's hot out here." But Roscoe ignored her and ambled over to the water bowl. He lapped the water for a minute and then stretched out in the shaded grass next to the igloo. "All right. I guess you know what you want. I know I want air conditioning."

Rose gave the cat a tickle and turned to go back in when her neighbor came around the side of the house next door dragging a garden hose. She stopped at a large rhododendron that had clearly seen better days and turned the nozzle on.

Rose called, "Mrs. Hudson, how are you today? You shouldn't be out here. It's too hot."

"I just popped out to water my plants and then I'm right back in to the air conditioning. But I can't let them dry up, especially this one. It had a hard winter and I'd like to save it. I planted it when we moved in, nearly fifty years ago."

"You'll save it. You've got the gardener's touch. Did I see your niece on the porch the other day?"

"Yes. Abby's here for the summer. The family is worried

7

about me being here alone and she has the summer off. She teaches, you know. So she was elected to babysit."

"I'm sure she loves the time with you. You two should come for dinner soon. I haven't really had a chance to get to know her."

"That would be nice. I'm afraid Abby might be a little bit bored. There isn't a great deal for her to do other than look after me."

"Well, let me talk to Daisy and we'll set something up. Now get your watering done and get back inside."

"Mrs. Hudson's niece is staying for the summer." Rose opened the safe, took out the cash box, and put it in the register. "I thought we could have them over for dinner one night."

"That would be nice. Do you know anything about her? Abigail, right? I don't even know her last name."

"Wentworth. I've only met her a few times. She stayed with Mrs. H. the last few summers for a couple of weeks in June. I thought you had met her too."

Daisy said, "I must have been on vacation."

"Well, she's nice enough. A little goofy, but who isn't? She didn't say much about herself, but she seems fond of Mrs. H."

"Maybe we should make it a party."

"A small party would be nice. We could cook-out." Rose took a large gulp of her iced tea she'd left on the counter and fanned herself with the newspaper. "And eat in."

A few minutes later a key turned in the door and their assistant, Tonya Albert, walked in and said, "My, it's hot out there!"

Daisy asked, "I know it. How do you manage to look so good in this heat?"

Tonya looked cool and elegant in the butter colored blouse and slacks that set off her beautiful coffee-with-cream complexion and dark eyes.

Tonya laughed. "Do I? Thanks. I have no idea. I thought I'd melt just walking in from the car."

Daisy smiled as she watched Tonya turn the door sign to OPEN, pick up a cloth and quickly wipe smudges off the glass, and then de-clutter the counter. She and Rose had certainly been lucky to find her.

Tonya said, "I just saw a man in The Book Renew. Is that the new owner? Have you met him?"

Rose looked up from the bills she was sorting and said, "Sort of. He slammed a door in my face and I dropped his Express Mail in a puddle. He has very lovely eyes."

Tonya laughed. "Sounds about right. Mom says he's single and paid cash for the place."

Daisy rolled her eyes and said, "Mary's grapevine hard at work. I thought I might go over there and say hi this afternoon. You want to come with me, Rose?"

"Maybe. I'll see how I feel."

They were waiting for Angela Forrest when Tom Willis walked in. Daisy smiled and said, "Tonya, your policeman is here. How are you, Tom? How's crime?"

Tom Willis was a Bostwick city policeman whom they got to know quite well late last year when Old Towne was center ring in a lunatic's circus. He and Tonya had fallen in love over Thanksgiving dinner and had been an item ever since.

"Very slow. Not much more going on other than kids being rowdy."

"Great! I like a quiet, little town. Oh, look, Mother just pulled up. Well, we're off to lunch. You can have Tonya all to yourself."

Angela with Percy in tow threw open the shop door and cried, "Come out here. Quick. You'll miss him."

"What?" They followed her out and stood on the steps

watching Angela look up and down the street.

"Oh, rats, he's gone," said Angela as she turned to go back into the shop.

"Who's gone?" asked Daisy following.

"The man jogging along with his doo-watty hanging out! Can you believe it? What a hoot!"

Tom Willis bounded out the door and started down the street.

"Really? A streaker? Mother, are you sure?"

"Of course, I'm sure. I know a doodle when I see one. I was married for quite a long time, you know. But I don't think he was actually streaking. His privates just seemed to have escaped his pants. And he wasn't going very fast. Just, you know, bob-bob-bobbing along. Why did Tom run out of here so quickly?"

Tonya started laughing. "Apparently, this guy has been busy exposing himself all over town for the last few weeks and the police can't catch him. I guess it's not really funny. He could be dangerous, but so far all he's been doing is jogging along with his boys hanging out and disappearing before anyone can grab him."

Tom came back and said, "If I get my hands on that guy, he'll be sorry. I'm sorry you had to see that, Ms. Forrest."

"Call me Angela. Not to worry, Tom. I think it's kind of funny. I mean, I only caught a short glimpse, but he didn't seem to have that much to be proud of!"

Rose laughed and said, "Okay, the excitement seems to be over and I'm hungry. Are we ready for lunch? And Mother, I think we'll leave the doggies here. They'll be happier and so will I."

They walked across the street to the Clover Tavern. The lunch rush was in full swing and there was a short wait.

They were alone in the reception area looking at artwork by a few local painters when the phone on the front desk rang. Mattie Clover, who owned the Tavern with her husband Frank, hurried in from the bar to answer it. She murmured a few words, then she slowly replaced the receiver.

Rose looked over and Mattie was just standing there, staring out the window with tears running down her cheeks.

"Mattie, what's wrong? Are you okay?"

Mattie jumped, wiped her eyes with a tissue and said, "Sorry. I didn't even see you there. I'm fine. Just, you know, nothing. I'm fine. Let me see about your table."

Chapter Two

At seven thirty the next morning Rose came up the stairs from the kitchen wearing an emerald green tank top that matched her eyes. Her long auburn hair was pulled back in a ponytail, a water bottle hung from her wrist.

"Hey, I'm ready to go. Are you coming?"

"Just a sec," called Daisy.

"What are you doing, Daisy? It's getting hotter by the minute and you know I hate to get too sweaty."

Rose stuck her head around the bedroom door just as Daisy was brushing color onto her cheeks.

Daisy looked up and said, "One minute. Mascara and lip gloss and I'm all yours."

"Holy catfish! You're putting make-up on to go walking in this heat?"

"You never know who you'll meet. I don't want to scare anyone." She finished her make-up and pulled her curly, blond hair into a loose knot.

"Daisy, you're nuts. You look fine."

"You think? I went out to get the paper the other morning and the paperboy asked if I'd died recently."

"He's just an annoying kid."

"Well, I feel old age creeping up on me. You and I are staring late thirties in the face and I don't like it. A little make-up makes me feel younger."

"Oh, just come on. It's already eighty degrees."

They left the house with Malcolm on his leash and headed for the bike trail that ran behind their property.

Rose stretched her arms and breathed in deeply. "I think this is the best part of my day."

Daisy adjusted the blue bandana that was holding her curls in place. "This is good, but I think the best part of my day is the seven p.m. vodka tonic. So civilized and decidedly un-sweaty."

They walked in silence for a while enjoying the breeze that cooled the air slightly. Then Daisy said, "I wonder why Mattie was upset yesterday. She's usually so upbeat. I don't think I've ever seen her down, much less in tears."

"I know. She seems really distracted lately. And she didn't make the last Chamber of Commerce meeting. That's unheard of."

"Maybe she's sick. Or maybe Frank is."

"I hope not. That would be terrible!"

The sisters walked along the path, Daisy humming songs from *Mama Mia*. Suddenly, she burst out into "Dancing Queen" and went skipping down the path with Malcolm right beside her.

"You look like an idiot!" Rose laughed as she caught up with her.

"Perhaps. But an idiot full of joie de vivre, don't you think?" asked Daisy as she continued dancing down the path, her neon pink *I Got My Crabs from Dirty Dick's Crab House* tee shirt billowing in the breeze.

"You're certainly full of something. Malcolm, come back here." Malcolm had run further ahead and was humping the mile marker in a desultory sort of way. He turned and started back toward Rose, then stopped and darted off toward the trees.

"Malcolm, not there. Get back here. Daisy, get your dog."

Daisy looked to where Malcolm was digging in the brush. "Oh, Malcolm. Come here, boy."

She turned to Rose. "That's where we found Ted Williamson's body last year. We shouldn't come this way. I think it upsets him."

Rose said, "It upsets me too, when I think about it. But I'm not going to give up walking a perfectly good path because of that. Just go get him and we'll go home."

"Malcolm, come here, you hairy fool." Daisy started to wade through the tall grass, then stopped. "You don't think he's found another body, do you? That would be too weird."

"No." Rose hesitated, "I mean, no. No. No body. Probably just some old bone." Rose put her hand to her mouth and said, "Ooh, I hope not a bone."

Malcolm started barking and wagging his tail.

Daisy finally reached the dog and attached his leash. "Well, he's found something." She bent down, picked up a black canvas tote bag, and carried it to the path with Malcolm in tow.

Daisy looked into it and said, "It's mail."

"A small man?"

"Yes. A teeny, weenie man. No, actually it seems to be mail. Letters." She pulled one out. "Hey, this is ours. Why is our mail lying in the bushes?"

"Beats me. Maybe that old bat, Peggy, has gone completely around the bend and is playing hide and seek with the post. I'm glad we found it. But now I'll have to go to the post office and find out what's going on."

They got back to Champagne Taste, put Malcolm in the backyard, and entered the house through the private entrance on the far end of the front porch. Daisy threw the tote onto the small table in the entry hall, and she and Rose ran upstairs to get showers. Dressed and re-made-up Daisy came down the stairs and opened the door in the small hallway that led directly into the shop.

Roscoe had pulled the tote off the little table and was batting it for all he was worth.

"What's the deal, Roscoe? Is there a tiny, little mailman in there?"

As she lifted the cat and started scratching his tummy, the tote caught on Roscoe's paw and everything spilled out.

Daisy muttered "Oops," then let out an earsplitting scream as a sinewy, black body slithered through the letters toward her foot. She dropped Roscoe with a thud and jumped back up the stairs.

Rose ran down the stairs and collided with Daisy. "What are you screaming about?"

"Snake! Snake! Right there. It's a snake," screamed Daisy putting a vise-grip on Rose's arm and pointing to the table.

"Hells bells! How did a snake get in here?"

"I think we carried it home in that tote bag. What do we do now?"

"First, you let go of my arm. You're cutting off the circulation."

"Oh, sorry. I don't like snakes."

"Well, where is it?" asked Rose as she cautiously crept down the stairs.

Daisy pointed and said, "Right there, next to the table." Only it wasn't. "Oh my God, where is it!"

"Holy mackerel, we have a snake on the loose. Where's Roscoe?"

The question wasn't out of her mouth when Roscoe walked in from the shop with something black and slinky wriggling in his mouth. He walked up to Rose and dropped it at her feet where it lay for a moment apparently contemplating its fate. Then it started slithering again.

"Roscoe, pick that thing up," she yelled as she jumped back onto the staircase colliding with Daisy for a second time. Daisy screamed again even louder and tripped over her own feet almost knocking Rose down the steps.

"Oh for God's sake, cut it out, would you?" cried Rose as she caught herself.

"Sorry. Again. I just really don't like snakes," said Daisy.

"And I do? We need to be calm."

Roscoe gave them a baleful stare. Then he picked the snake

up in his mouth again and sat there waiting for instructions.

"Okay, Roscoe. Outside. Take it outside. NOW!" Rose ordered as she darted past the cat and the snake and pushed open the outside door, then jumped back to the steps. But Roscoe just hunkered down with the snake under his paw teasing the poor thing.

"Look. He's grinning at us," said Rose. "Go. Get. Take your friend outside."

There was a tap on the door and a man poked his head in. "You need some help? I heard someone screaming."

"Brad! Hi. A little snake problem. We seem to have brought one home with us and Roscoe apparently wants to adopt it. Daisy and I aren't too hot on the idea, and we're having trouble convincing him to let it go."

He looked down. Roscoe had the snake in his mouth again and was heading back to the shop.

"Stop him!"

In a swift motion Brad caught Roscoe under the legs and pried the hapless reptile out of his jaws. Holding it behind its head, he took it outside.

A minute later he came back in. "All taken care of. Relax. It was only a little black snake. They're harmless."

"So I've heard. Still, snakes! Ghastly," replied Daisy with a shudder. "I'm so glad you were passing. We might have been sitting on these steps all day. Thanks for the help. How have you been, anyway? I haven't seen you around lately."

Brad Douglas had moved in a little over a year ago and opened a sports memorabilia shop called Yesterday's Heroes. He still looked like the running back he had been in college: five-ten, stocky, no neck– with curly dark hair and a mischievous smile.

"I've been in and out going to yard sales and memorabilia shows. And I've been umpiring Babe Ruth and Boy's Club baseball."

Rose smiled, "Have you? That must be fun. Or is it a pain in the neck?"

"It's okay. The kids are great. The parents can be pretty insane. But the extra money comes in handy."

"Always! Would you like some iced tea? I'm buying."

"No, thanks. I've got to get the store opened. How did that snake get in here anyway?"

Daisy picked up the tote bag. "Would you believe we carried him home in this thing? Malcolm found it lying in the bushes. The strangest part is it was full of our mail."

She bent to gather up the letters lying on the floor, but Brad beat her to it and scooped them up.

Daisy said, "We're going to have to talk with the wicked witch of the east and find out why there was a tote bag with our letters lying on the side of the bike path."

"The wicked witch? You mean that woman at the post office, don't you? You're right about that. This mail thing is weird, all right. Well, good luck with it. See you later."

He dropped the letters back into the tote and left.

Rose said, "Come on. We're late. We need to get the shop open."

Daisy dumped the mail onto the counter and was sorting through it. She burst out angrily, "This is a wedding invitation! How did it get in this stupid bag?"

Rose said, "I don't know. It doesn't make any sense, at all." Roscoe jumped up on the counter and sniffed the bag. Rose looked at it suspiciously. "Are you sure it's empty?"

Daisy shook the tote out. "Yep. No more snakes."

Rose picked Roscoe up and said, "You were no help, buddy, and you're lucky Brad came by." said Rose. "He's such a nice guy. And I love his shop. Sometimes those sports memorabilia places are kind of junky. But his is beautiful and I think a lot of what he has is pretty valuable."

"I know," answered Daisy. "He was showing me his Mickey Mantle rookie card. It's autographed and dated. He says it's worth a small fortune."

"I guess to somebody who cares, maybe. It wouldn't be worth much to me."

"Well, to someone who cares it's apparently worth about a quarter of a million dollars. I looked it up on the internet and that's what one sold for not too long ago."

Rose's eyebrows shot up. "Holy banana peels. What people will spend their money on is amazing! Well, I'm going over to Flowers and Finery for fresh flowers. Want anything while I'm out?"

Rose and Daisy liked to have flowers in the sunroom. And not being much in the way of gardeners, they usually got them from the florist across the bridge.

"Get sunflowers if Sally has them. Or spider mums. And maybe a doughnut."

"Okeydokey."

Rose came back a little later, sunflowers and a bag of doughnuts in hand. "Something weird must be going around. I walked into Sally's shop and she was crying. I asked her what was wrong and she sounded just like Mattie the other day. You know, 'Nothing's wrong. I'm fine. Let me get your flowers.'"

"That's just odd. Maybe their businesses aren't doing well. Maybe they both invested money in something and it fell through."

"Or maybe they were each having a bad day and we should mind our own business."

Daisy huffed, "Minding our own business is highly overrated. Besides, they're our friends. We should help if we can."

"Daisy, you know the kind of trouble your help has gotten you into before. Let's just let Mattie and Sally handle their problems by themselves."

"Oh, all right. But, you're no fun at all. Did you know that?"

"Maybe not. But I make a mean Mai Tai which is on the menu for cocktail hour and if you're not nice to me, you're not getting one!"

Chapter Three

Early Friday morning Rose stood outside the post office bracing herself for a fight. Mattie Clover came up beside her and said, "Hi. What's up? You look kind of lost."

Rose smiled and said, "Not lost. Just cowardly. I have a complaint for Peggy and I'm procrastinating."

"I know how you feel. The other day I was looking for a Next Day Letter I should have gotten. It wasn't in my box, so I asked her if she had it in the back. She screamed at me that she'd sort the mail when she felt like it. I always think of Hansel and Gretel when I come here. The building is so lovely, but an evil witch lives inside."

The small, white clapboard cottage with brick-red shingled roof was encircled by a low yew hedge. Red geraniums and candy-cane striped petunias bloomed in window boxes, and the winding brick path leading to the door was lined with beautiful pink and yellow roses.

"You're right. That's exactly what it feels like. Well, here goes. If you see her pop me into an oven, call Daisy and tell her she's on her own."

"Will do," said Mattie laughing.

Inside the post office looked like any other. Mail boxes lined the wall on the left. The right wall was covered with shelves holding shipping boxes, envelopes and labels. A small counter sat in the middle of the room for customer use.

Peggy didn't really look like a witch. About five foot two with short grey hair and frown lines, but no warts, she sat behind a counter that stretched the width of the cottage reading a Harlequin romance and looking decidedly unpleasant, as usual.

Mattie walked over to the boxes and got out her key as Rose approached the counter.

"Peggy, hi. How are you today?"

She looked up from her book and squinted suspiciously at Rose. "Why?"

"Just being sociable. I have a little problem that I'm hoping you can help me with."

"What now? Seems like everybody's got a problem. And they all want me to fix it."

"Well, this one concerns our mail. Daisy and I found a tote bag on the bike path yesterday that was full of it. Our mail, I mean. I was just wondering how it got there."

"How the hell should I know? What you do with your mail after I put it in your box isn't my problem."

"But it never got into our box. That's the trouble. How could our mail get dumped onto the side of the path? I think that's probably illegal, isn't it?"

"What? You think I have time to go dumping mail all around. What kind of fool are you?"

Rose was keeping her temper, but just barely. Mattie was watching them, holding her letters in one hand and her cell phone in the other, in case she needed to call for help.

"Peggy, is it possible that you put our mail into the wrong box? Or that it was left outside or something?"

"No!"

"No? No!" Rose's voice was rising slightly. "In all the years you've worked here, you've never put a freaking piece of mail into the wrong box?"

"No. What are you trying do, you little bitch, get me fired?"

"Peggy, I'm just trying to find out why my mail was thrown into the woods. I'd think you'd want to know, too. After all, the mail is your responsibility."

"Not after it leaves this building, it's not. Now you just get the hell out of here and let me get back to work." She picked up her book and stalked to the back room.

Rose stood still and counted to twenty. Then counted again. She took a deep breath and then went over to Box 769 to get the mail for Champagne Taste. Mattie was at the counter going through hers. When Rose turned to leave she saw Mattie standing at the counter with tears running down her face.

"Mattie, something's wrong. What is it? Can I help?"

Mattie wiped her eyes with a tissue and said, "No. Thanks. Nothing's wrong. Just a bad day. I'm just having a bad day." She turned and left the post office.

Rose was in her living room sifting through the mail she had just retrieved and sighed. She called up the stairs to Daisy. "That woman is becoming a real nuisance! Now we have Brad's letters in our box. I'm going to walk them over to his shop. Want to come?"

"Sure. I'll be down in a minute."

They were a couple of doors away from Yesterday's Heroes when they saw Peter Fleming going in.

"Oh, good. We'll get to meet the man officially," said Daisy.

"It had to happen sometime. Here goes!" Rose said as she pulled open the door. The walls of the small shop were covered with shelves containing all sorts of sports memorabilia: jerseys, helmets, trading cards, bats, balls, hundreds of autographed pictures. Brad was sitting behind the glass counter in the back where he kept the most expensive items under lock and key. Rose called out, "Hey, Brad. I'm just bringing you some of your mail. It was in our box."

She walked past Peter Fleming and put five envelopes on the counter. Brad smiled and said, "Thanks. This is getting to be a real pain," as he picked them up and took a quick look.

"So how're you doing? No more snakes, I hope?"

"No. We seem to be completely snake-free. I'm sure you'll hear me screaming if we're not."

Brad laughed and said, "Hey, have you two met Pete? This is Pete Fleming, our new neighbor. He bought the book store.

"Pete, meet Daisy and Rose Forrest. They own Champagne Taste."

"Peter." Peter smiled politely and said, "We haven't met exactly. Rose kindly retrieved a letter that I dropped, though it got damp in the process."

Rose smiled in return and said, "Sorry about that. I was hot."

"No, I'm the one who should be sorry. I was abominably rude. I hope you'll let me make it up to you. Maybe I could buy you a cup of coffee?"

"Sure, if you could make it lemonade instead."

"Lemonade it is. Whenever you're free."

Rose thought for a minute and looked at Daisy who just raised her eyebrows and smiled.

"Well, actually, I'm free this morning."

"Good. Perhaps we could try the Tavern."

"We could. It's nice."

Rose glanced out the window and saw a young woman jogging up the street, bright blue walking weights in her hands and a water bottle strapped to her waist.

"Lord love a duck, look at that. Who in her right mind would run at this time of day?"

The woman looked into the window and stopped running. Then she opened the shop door and came in. She was cute in an athletic sort of way, in her late twenties, short with red, curly hair and freckles.

"Wow, I cannot believe how hot it is," she panted. "Too hot to be jogging really, but I don't want to get out of shape." She looked at Brad and cooed, "Is it all right if I cool off in here?"

Brad grinned, "Abby! Sure, come on in. I was hoping you'd stop by again. Abby and I met the other day. She's staying with

Mrs. Hudson."

Daisy gave her a smile. "Of course. Sarah Hudson's niece. I'm Daisy and this is my sister Rose. We're your neighbors."

"Oh, sure. I met Rose last summer."

"And this is Peter Fleming. He's the new kid on the block."

Peter gave a nod.

Rose said, "I just saw Sarah the other day. I think she's afraid you're bored with nothing to do but look after her."

"She's crazy. I love being with her. And I've already made some friends. And Brad has been so nice." She planted a big, wet one on his cheek. "And don't you just love this shop?"

Brad smiled like an idiot and Daisy elbowed Rose and whispered, "Did you bring a barf bag?"

Rose whispered back, "I think she's cute."

Peter Fleming turned away from the public display of affection and looked around the shop. He spotted a curio box hanging behind the counter and said, "Is that Mantle's rookie card?"

Rose looked at him in surprise. "You know baseball? I'm surprised." To Brad she said, "Daisy said you had a real collector's item. Is that it?"

Brad took the box down from the wall and put it on the counter.

"Yep. It's a family heirloom."

"You really shouldn't keep this in here. It must be worth a fortune. It's in absolutely mint condition."

"I know. I put it in the safe at night. But I figure what's the point of having something like this if you hide it away. It's something else, huh?"

"As you say, it's a real treasure!"

Abby cried, "I love Mickey Mantle."

Daisy said, "Of course you do." Brad grinned like a school kid.

Rose gave Daisy a look and said, "We'd better be going.

Come on Peter, I'm getting thirsty."

Brad said, "Thanks for bringing my mail by. I think that old lady is really losing it!"

They were almost out the door when Rose turned and said, "I told your aunt we'd have a sort of get-to-know-you dinner for you. How about Sunday? We'll cook out. And if Peter can make it too, you could both meet some of the neighbors."

"Sunday's good for me," said Brad. Abby nodded.

Peter said, "I do happen to be free. That would be very nice."

"Great. Sunday, six o'clock, burgers on the grill."

Daisy, Rose and Peter Fleming left Brad showing Abby around the shop and started down the street toward the Tavern.

As they walked Daisy asked Peter, "Is that card of Brad's really worth a lot?"

"I believe so."

"Wow. You know, he showed it to me the other day and it looked different. The colors looked darker."

Peter smiled and said, "It was probably the light. I don't think he'd have two of them!"

Daisy said, "Me neither. And what do I know about baseball cards anyway? Not a thing."

They got to the corner and Daisy turned toward Champagne Taste.

Peter said, "Daisy, I hope you'll join us."

"I'd love to, but I'm working this afternoon and need to get a few things done."

"You want me to bring you something?" asked Rose.

"No, thanks. I'm good." She waved and veered off toward the shop.

Mattie was at the reception desk looking only marginally better than she did the day before. She smiled when she saw Rose and was introduced to Peter.

"It's always nice to have some new blood in the area. Will you keep the shop as it is? Or will you be heading in a different direction?"

"Well, this is really going to be a hobby and I must admit feeling a bit like a dilettante around all you hard working professionals. For now I'm just going to keep it as it is."

Rose smiled and said, "I don't think anyone here would consider you a dilettante. After all you're a hard working professor of... English? That would certainly be book related. And really, we're just happy the shop isn't sitting empty."

"We are that," said Mattie as she led them to a corner booth. "I'm glad we met. I hope you enjoy your meal."

As Rose and Peter sat down, she asked, "Was I right? You teach English?"

"Sorry, no. Philosophy. How do you know I teach at all?"

"Small town, big grapevine. You will have no secrets here."

"I see. Well, I spend my time trying to encourage young minds to consider diverse ideas. However, I find that most are so entrenched in their own popular culture that the musings of Sartre or Plato, or even Christ for that matter, are of little interest. Perhaps I'm asking too much."

"Well, you are probably making more of an impact on them than you think. It amazes me how much I remember from college. And, Lord knows, I wasn't the most serious student on the campus."

"More interested in culturally deficient old movies, I assume."

"Huh?"

"*Rocky*? I'm sure you must have had some higher aspirations."

"Oh, I did. I aspired to fool around with my fiancé in every building on campus. And I will have you know, we almost did. When push came to shove though, we drew the line at the chapel. That just didn't seem right."

"You had a sexual encounter in every building?"

"Well, it was a small campus. Boy, you make it sound so

clinical. We were just young and in love and having a lot of fun."

"Are you serious? I find that rather appalling."

"I am serious. Are you? You never went to parties? Got a little looped?"

He shook his head. "I've always taken life quite seriously."

"That must be tiring." Rose sat up straight and did a little wavy thing with her fingers. "Well, this is good. Getting to know each other. I really am sorry about the other morning. I was hot and I shouldn't have thrown your letter in the puddle."

"True. Apology accepted."

A waitress came over to the table and Peter said, "A lemonade and a black coffee. No need to bring any cream or sugar."

"Oh, sorry. I've changed my mind," chirped Rose. "Iced tea with lemon. And I'd love some sugar."

The waitress smiled and said, "I'll get that right away."

"I thought you wanted lemonade. I don't like sudden changes."

"Sudden changes? Oh. Well, it's not like I suddenly changed into a man or something. You're a bit inflexible, aren't you? Just a thought, but if you lightened up a little, maybe your students would take more interest."

Their waitress put their drinks on the table and asked, "Anything else?"

"I don't think so, but let me check." Peter looked at Rose and asked, "Rose, do you care for anything else?" He sounded snippy.

She smiled. "No, I'm just ducky. Thanks." The waitress left and Peter continued, "So you think I should lower my standards and teach pop philosophy? I really don't understand that kind of thinking."

"I never said you should lower your standards. I'm just thinking like a twenty year old."

"Well, you should be thinking like an adult." His voice was rising. "And so should they. That is what these students should be. Adults. But they are coddled and spoiled by their parents and society. And now you want me to do the same."

"You sure listen with an accent. I never said anything like that." She spoke slowly and quietly.

"I believe you did."

"Did not." Rose was holding two packets of sugar over her tea.

"I guess a woman who spent her college years in pursuit of carnal pleasures would think that way."

Rose stood up calmly. "Carnal pleasures? That's a really stuffy way of putting it. Well, it's been great getting to know you. Enjoy your coffee." She dumped the sugar into Peter's cup, turned and walked out of the restaurant.

Chapter Four

"I cannot believe what I did! I told him all about Paul! I hardly know the man and I'm not sure I even like him. Why would I do that?"

Rose was sitting in the sunroom sipping lemonade and sighing while Daisy opened that morning's mail.

"You told him about Paul? Well, it's a little early to bring up your ex, but he'd have to find out sometime. You didn't start crying or anything, did you?"

"Crying? No. Oh! No, I didn't tell him about the biggest heartbreak of my life. I told him that we fooled around in almost every building on campus! He must think I'm a total slut."

"I never knew you did that. With Paul?"

"What? Of course, with Paul. Who did you think I'd be fooling around with? The football team?"

Daisy started laughing. "I'll bet you got his attention. Isn't that what you wanted? He is handsome and the snobby stuff could just be nerves. New place, new people. I'll bet he's really a nice guy when he's relaxed."

"I'm not sure the man relaxes, and I don't think I'll ever find out. I doubt he'll want to see me again. I got mad and dumped sugar in his coffee. Then I walked out in a huff."

"So either he's kicking himself right now for being a jerk. Or he's not. Nothing you can do about it."

Daisy started laughing. "You and Paul! The whole campus. I love it. Even the heating plant? I could never find a way in."

Suddenly she let out a yelp. "Wow! Look at this!"

She and Rose were staring at a pile of bills, mostly fives and tens, and some twenties that Daisy had just taken out of a large manila envelope.

Rose started counting. "Holy mother of pearl, there's almost a thousand dollars here." She took the envelope and looked at the label. "We have to put this back. It's not ours."

"Well, whose is it?"

Rose looked at the envelope. "I don't know. It's been forwarded, and the name on the label is smeared. But it's to Box 768, the one right next to ours. Peggy must have put it in our box by mistake."

Daisy said, "Maybe there's a note or something."

Rose said, "It doesn't matter. Just put it all back and we'll take it over to the post office tomorrow. This is not our business."

Daisy said, "It won't hurt to find out who should get this. We can return it to them directly." She shook the envelope and a slip of paper fell onto the table.

"Uh-oh. This doesn't sound too good. 'This is all I have. I can't come up with any more. Do whatever you're going to do.'" She looked at Rose and said, "What do you think?"

"I don't know." She took the note from Daisy and looked at it. "Maybe I just have a really suspicious nature, but this sounds like it could be blackmail money. Is that crazy?"

Rose put the note on the table. Then she picked it up again and looked more closely. "This is bad. I'm pretty sure Mattie Clover wrote this."

"How can you tell?"

Rose walked over to her desk and pulled a sheet of paper from a folder. "Here. Mattie's organizing the Fourth of July picnic. She gave me this to-do list. Look. The handwriting's the same."

Daisy studied the list. "You're right. Well, clearly something is going on. And it's not anything good. What should we do?"

"I'm not sure. Maybe talk to Mattie and see if we can help in some way. You know, I wonder..."

"What? You wonder what?" asked Daisy.

"Well, if someone is blackmailing Mattie, maybe they're blackmailing other people too."

Daisy said, "You're thinking of Sally Henderson, aren't you? I think you're making a bit of an assumption here. We don't know if this is blackmail. We don't know who Mattie was sending money to or why. It could be anything, a sick relative. Who knows?"

"I think we have to talk to Mattie. What else can we do?"

Late Friday afternoon Daisy said, "Mother called and said she'd be here by 7:30. We'd better get changed. She's been looking forward to this all week." A Hitchcock retrospective was playing at the Dupont Theatre in downtown Washington.

"Which movie?" Rose asked.

"Her favorite, *Spellbound*." They heard a car door and Daisy said, "Speak of the pixilated angel. She's early."

"Are my girls ready for a night out?" Angela called as she came tripping into the shop through the hall door. "You really should keep your front door locked, you know."

She stood in the doorway wearing a flowing, mid-calf length, belted, green shirtwaist dress with shoulder pads and matching green peep-toe heels. Her golden hair was pulled up on the sides into rolls held with tortoiseshell-colored combs.

"You look lovely and so very 1940's. You're putting us to shame. We'll be ready in a couple of minutes," said Rose looking down at the shorts and tee shirt she had been wearing all afternoon.

"Well, hurry up. The show starts at eight-thirty and we need time to get popcorn."

A few minutes later Daisy and Rose came down the stairs looking cool and comfortable. Rose was wearing a yellow and white flowered shift and Daisy had on a blue voile tunic that brought out the blue of her eyes and white capris. As they were leaving Daisy said, "Just a sec," and ran back into the office.

"All set," she said putting something into her purse.

Rose asked, "What's that?"

"Nothing. I'll drive."

They hopped into Daisy's ruby red Subaru and headed to Washington, D.C. Rush hour was winding down, and most of the traffic was leaving the city. Traffic going south as they drove along Piney Branch Road was practically non-existent.

Daisy said, "Wow, this is spooky. I feel like Jeff Goldblum and Judd Hirsch in *Independence Day* driving into Washington on that empty road, as everybody in the entire city is pouring out of it on the other side of the highway."

Rose chimed in, "Which was always a problem for me. I mean, really, if everybody and his mother is trying to escape alien creatures who are about to blow us all to smithereens, would we all be so law-abiding that we wouldn't be using both sides of the highway? That's just silly."

"But if people had done that, Jeff Goldblum wouldn't have been able to save the world and we wouldn't be here to go to a movie this evening, would we?" asked Angela.

Daisy looked sideways at her mother and said, "It wasn't real, Mother. It was a movie."

"Well, yes, but you never know, do you?"

Having no answer to that, Daisy just shook her head and turned onto Sixteenth Street, NW. They cruised down Sixteenth and finally cut through Adams Morgan on Columbia Road, turning left onto Connecticut Avenue.

They were approaching Dupont Circle when Rose pointed to her right and said, "Parking lot right there."

"There's a small detour I want to make first." She continued to the Circle, veered off onto P Street, made a quick left onto 20th Street and pulled over to the curb.

She took a piece of paper out of her pocket and read "1421. There it is."

"What is?" asked Rose.

Just as Daisy pointed out the window to a beautiful brick row-house near the corner, she hissed, "Get down. He'll see us."

As Rose automatically ducked her head she hissed back, "Who will see us?"

Angela sat up straight and looked out the window. "Is it the 'bobber' again? Where?"

"Mother, why would the 'bobber' be here? No. It's Peter Fleming coming out of his door. That's where he lives."

"Daisy, are you nuts? What, we're in high school again driving past boys' houses?"

Daisy whispered, "Oh come on, Rose. You know you're curious about the man. And since we were down here anyway, I thought we'd just explore. Has he gone, Mother?"

"Not really," answered Angela as she rolled down the window and said, "Why, hello there."

Daisy sat up with a jerk and looked at Peter Fleming's handsome face peering in the window. He said, "I thought I saw you over here. This is certainly a surprise. Is something wrong? You look a bit lost."

Rose sat up with what dignity she could muster and said, "Oh no, not lost. We're going to see Hitchcock at the Dupont. I was hunting for my umbrella." She held up a tightly rolled blue mini-brella."

He looked at the cloudless blue sky and said, "It's not raining."

"Well, you can never be too careful. Summer storms can be so unpredictable."

He nodded. "Yes they can."

"Oh gee. How about that!" said Daisy. "Better get a move on or we'll miss the beginning. *Spellbound*, a classic. Great to see you. You're still coming to dinner Sunday, aren't you?"

"Certainly. Until then," said Peter with a bewildered look on his face.

Daisy pulled away from the curb and Rose moaned, "Good God Almighty! I cannot believe you did that. This is too embarrassing."

"I don't know. I think that umbrella business was pretty good. I'm sure he bought it."

"You bet. We just happen to be sitting across from his house with our heads in our laps while Mother's looking for a naked man and I feel a thunderstorm coming on. Yes, I'm sure he thinks we're perfectly normal."

Angela chirped, "Who is this Peter Fleming?"

Daisy said, "He bought the Book Renew and he and Rose have been exchanging insults for the last couple of days."

"Wonderful. He has very nice eyes, Rose. And his home is lovely."

Sunday evening the weather let up a bit and it was a balmy eighty-five degrees when the party got together for cocktails. In addition to Brad, Abby, Mrs. Hudson, and Angela, the sisters invited Marc Proctor, Daisy's mostly off-again boyfriend, and their neighbor, Ron Tucker.

At six-thirty Peter Fleming came around the side of the house carrying a bouquet of freesia and roses. Rose took the flowers and smiled, "These are gorgeous. Thank you so much. Have a drink while I put these in a vase."

Daisy made the introductions. Then she handed him a tall glass of golden liquid with a little palm tree sticking out of it and said, "Pearl Harbor?"

"Pearl Harbor?" he asked a bit doubtfully.

"Just a little cocktail to get you bombed!" Peter looked slightly startled and Daisy said, "That's a joke."

"Ah. Yes, a drink would be fine. How was the film?"

"Oh, you know. Gregory Peck. Ingrid Bergman. What more do you need?"

"Indeed. But I think I prefer the chemistry in *Indiscreet* with

Cary Grant and Ingrid."

"Well, if we're going to compare the merits of Cary Grant and Gregory Peck – we should have a debate on all of Ingrid's leading men."

Peter lifted his glass and lisped, "Yesh, we should shweetheart."

Daisy laughed and said, "What a great Bogart! You're very talented." Peter blushed and said, "I taught a classic film class one semester. How did you and Rose come to be so interested in old films?"

"We didn't have much choice. Mother loves them and dragged us to every theatre that ran them. Now we go willingly."

As the evening moved on and Peter had another drink or two, he loosened up considerably. Rose couldn't believe it when he just patted Malcolm's head and muttered, "He's an excitable little fellow, isn't he?" when the dumb chum greeted him with an enthusiastic leg-humping.

She smiled at the two of them and decided to apologize for the sugar incident. She was just starting to say something when Peter said, "Rose, I'm so sorry about the other morning. I admit I can be a bit stuffy at times."

"Can't we all! I'm sorry, too."

"Perhaps we could have dinner one evening and start over again."

"I'd like that."

Brad walked over and started talking about business. Conversation lulled a bit and Peter asked how he had come to have Mantle's rookie card.

"My dad got the card Mantle's first season in the bigs and then got him to sign it in 1953 when the Yanks came to town to play the old Senators in Griffith Stadium. It was my Dad's birthday and he asked Mantle to hit a home run for him. And he did! That was the day The Mick hit that tape measure homerun off Chuck Stobbs. Five hundred and sixty-five feet! Dad even kept his ticket stub and score card, so we keep them all together. It's kind of a family heirloom now."

"If you don't mind my asking, have you had it valued?"

"Sure. Quite a few times. There's a really big show on the Outer Banks that I take it to every year to see if a serious buyer shows up. I don't know why really. I'd never sell it."

Abby took Brad's arm and said, "Of course you wouldn't. But it never hurts to know exactly what it's worth!"

Daisy was bringing out the dessert, a pear tart Angela had made that afternoon, when Mrs. Hudson said, "I have to run home for a minute. I have a letter for you."

She was back a couple of minutes later with a bill from one of their suppliers. "Here. This was delivered to me yesterday. It looks important."

Rose took the letter and said, "Thanks, Sarah. This is really getting nuts!"

"You haven't gotten any of my mail by any chance, have you? I was expecting something last week and it hasn't come."

"Sorry, no. If somebody else gets it, I'm sure they'll bring it to you."

"You're probably right. This tart looks wonderful!"

"Yoo hoo, anyone home?" called Daisy as she poked her head in the 'Private Entrance' door of the Tavern on Monday morning. They waited a minute and finally heard someone moving around in the kitchen.

She called a little louder. "Mattie, it's Daisy. You decent?"

A short, energetic woman came slowly out of the back of the restaurant. She looked hot as she brushed her short dark hair away from her face.

"Oh, Daisy. Rose. Hi. I was just cleaning the kitchen. It can get out of hand really quickly if I don't stay on top of it. But it's not my favorite job."

"Have you thought about hiring someone?" asked Rose.

"We had someone, but I had to let her go. We just don't have the money right now, unfortunately. Did you need something? Oh my God! Look at that!"

She had been looking out the open door and Daisy and Rose turned to see a man in a John Deere baseball cap, red tee shirt and black shorts running down the street toward them.

"That man's tallawacky is hanging out of his pants! What is wrong with people? I'm calling the police."

Just as she pulled out her cell phone the 'bobber' turned abruptly and started running toward the hiking trail.

Daisy ran outside and shouted, "Put that thing away, you moron. You've ruined my appetite!

"What a jerk. Tom Willis has been trying to catch the guy for weeks now. I guess you could call in another sighting, but they won't catch him now. Mother was right, though."

Mattie asked as she put her phone away, "About what?"

"She said he didn't have much to show off."

They all started laughing. But suddenly Mattie put her hands to her face and started to sob.

"Mattie, what's going on? Come on, I'll get some coffee and we'll sit down and figure it out."

Rose led Mattie into the dining room as Daisy went into the kitchen and poured coffee into three mugs. She brought them to a booth where Rose was holding Mattie's hand and waiting for her to calm down.

"I can't talk about it. I know you want to help, but you can't."

Rose took the money and note out of her bag and put it on the table. "Does it have anything to do with this?"

Mattie looked at the money and gasped. She pulled back from Rose and said, "You! You and Daisy? How could you? All these years we've been friends and...why would you do this to me?"

Daisy looked puzzled for a moment and then said, "Oh my God, Mattie. Not us. We just want to help you. We knew you must be in some kind of trouble."

Mattie shook her head. "I can't believe this is happening. I know people always say that, but I really can't. I'm so ashamed and embarrassed. Poor Frank doesn't know anything about it and I just can't tell him. How did you get this?"

"Just luck, really. You know how Peggy over at the post office has been getting everything mixed up lately. She put this in our box. And Rose recognized your handwriting."

"But I never sent anything to an address in Old Towne. The letter always says to mail it to Occupant at a suite number in Vienna, Maryland."

Rose said, "A suite number? So not the post office."

Mattie said, "No. Not the post office, but I don't know where it went. Or how it got here? I don't understand this."

"Look," Daisy took the envelope out and put it on the table. "It's been forwarded to Box 768 in Old Towne. I didn't even look at the label. I just opened it automatically. "

Rose said, "Mattie, what's going on? Begin at the beginning. Maybe we can help."

"Oh God, I should never have let it get this far. I don't know how anyone can help."

Mattie held her head in her hands and sighed. "I'm being blackmailed."

Rose said, "I was afraid it was something like that. But I can't imagine you doing anything blackmail worthy."

Mattie sniffled and wiped her nose with a tissue. "It goes back to when I was sixteen. I was a real mess. The whole teenage angst thing, hated my parents, all the usual stuff. I met this man. He was older, twenty-five, and I was flattered that he'd be interested in me. He was everything my parents hated–and rightly so - which I found out the hard way.

"He talked me into eloping with him. For our romantic honeymoon he took me to a little town with a nice bank which he robbed while I waited in the car. We were both caught."

She got up and stared out the window. "My parents got me a

decent lawyer and I ended up serving six months in a halfway house. The judge ruled that my record would be expunged when I was twenty-one assuming I behaved myself. My parents let me come back home afterward and I got an annulment.

"That's it. It was so long ago and I never told anyone. Not even Frank. We met at college and fell in love. That part of my life was over. I just wanted to pretend it never happened.

"Then about five years ago I got a letter in the mail asking for twenty-five dollars. It wasn't signed, so I just threw it out. The next week I got another one. This time it said 'I know about Wayne.' That was his name. 'Leave $25 in a brown paper bag in the grey trash bin at the farmers market on Saturday morning.'

"It was stupid. I shouldn't have agreed. I know I should have told Frank then, but it was only a couple of dollars. So I left it at the farmers market."

"And I guess that wasn't the end of it, was it?" asked Daisy.

"No. They never asked for much money. Never more than fifty. And not very often."

"Did you ever try to see who picked up the bag?"

"Sure, but I could never spot them. The drop-off was always some place really crowded like the farmers market. So I just gave up trying and paid."

She stopped talking and got up from the table. She walked to the window and stared at the quiet street.

"But then about two years ago the letters changed. They were nasty and threatening. I was to send the money to this address in Vienna Maryland. And they were demanding a lot more money.

"It's been so hard trying to hide this from Frank. I can't do it anymore. We're struggling to keep the restaurant open and he doesn't understand why. I keep the books and tell him all these lies about overhead and insurance and God knows what else. It's killing me.

"So I just told this person I'm through. I can't do anymore. I don't know what I'm going to do."

Rose looked thoughtful. "Well, first you're going to put this money back in the cash register. If you're going to stop paying this bastard you might as well stop now. Then, we'll try to figure out a way to catch this guy. It must be whoever rents Box 768. We just have to find out who that is."

"How? And then what? Go to the police?" asked Daisy.

"I don't know. But Mattie, I think you need to talk to Frank."

"I know. But could we keep the police out of it someway? It's so embarrassing. I'm not sure people would understand. Not only the stupid stuff I did when I was sixteen, but about paying the blackmail. I feel like an idiot."

"Okay, not the police. Not yet." Rose thought a moment. "Mattie, just sit tight. But talk to Frank. Daisy and I will try to figure something out."

Daisy said, "You could try to buy some time. Maybe you should re-send the letter and tell them you can't come up with the money right now. Ask if they'll wait for it? Something like that."

Rose took Mattie's hand and said, "That's a good idea. And if somehow we can figure out who's doing this, maybe we can make a deal. Sort of blackmail them back to keep them quiet.

Daisy said, "We'd better get a move on. Mattie, just talk to Frank and we'll talk later."

Chapter Five

Daisy said, "You know good and well Mattie has to go to the police. We can't let a blackmailer off."

"I know that, but I think Mattie needs a little time to figure that out for herself. And if we can find the person who's doing this, maybe we could figure someway to turn him in without Mattie being involved.

"And we need to talk to Sally Henderson. I think she might be another victim."

"Well, first things first. How can we find out who owns box 768?" asked Daisy.

"I don't think asking Peggy would do any good. Even if she were a nice person who might be inclined to help, she couldn't tell us that. She could get fired. But it doesn't really matter because she's not a nice person."

"We could stake out the box in Vienna."

"That wouldn't work. For one thing, it's two hours away from here. And secondly, the mail's being forwarded from there. The blackmailer probably never even goes near it. We could stake out our post office, but that could take forever and if the blackmailer has any sense at all, he wouldn't take anything out of the box when we were there. Come to think of it, I've never seen anyone use that box."

Daisy's eyes lit up. "There is one way we could find out."

Rose squinted her eyes. "No, we couldn't, Daisy. That's federal property. We are not breaking into the post office."

"You're no fun." She thought for a minute. "We wouldn't

have to break in. All we need to do is catch Peggy as she's opening up and distract her. You could keep her outside and I could sneak in and look through the book."

Rose said, "What book? Everything's on the computer, isn't it? We'd need her password and enough time to find the information."

"Nope. She's old-school. I know for a fact that she still keeps all the post office box information in a three ring binder. She used it when I went in to pay our bill last time."

"Well, that's something. What sort of distraction do think would work?"

As they were talking Roscoe bounded up the back stairs with Malcolm on his tail. He leapt onto the top of the bookcase and Malcolm set up as a sentry in front of it, barking out little doggie orders and shaking his paw at the cat.

They both looked at the dog and said, "Malcolm."

"Either Peggy likes dogs and plays with him or she hates dogs and Malcolm does his usual thing and really pisses her off," said Rose. "I'm betting on hating. She hates everyone else. Why would dogs be different?"

"Okay, we'll walk Malcolm over tomorrow morning at six thirty and wait. As soon as Peggy unlocks the door, but before she gets it open, you set Malcolm on her. I'll be lurking at the side and I'll slip in when she turns away. The timing has to be perfect. What do you think? I think it will work."

"I think if it doesn't work at least it will just be embarrassing, not criminal."

Early the next morning they waited. At five to seven Peggy still hadn't shown up.

"I knew something would screw this up," murmured Rose to a bush.

Daisy popped up and smacked her forehead and whispered, "I'll bet she uses the back door and is in there now. How stupid am I? Now what do we do?"

Rose shook her head. "I don't think she's here. I'd have heard something." She tried the door. "And she hasn't unlocked the door yet. She always opens at seven. Check around back and see if her car's there."

Daisy walked down the narrow alley on the far side of the building that led to the parking lot. Rose waited with Malcolm on the sidewalk. Then Daisy let out a scream.

Rose swore under her breath, "Great googlie-mooglie, Daisy. Be quiet. You'll attract the whole neighborhood."

She and Malcolm walked around the building. Daisy was standing there looking at a heap of dark blue clothes lying on the back doorstep of the post office.

"Oh my God," said Rose. Malcolm started whimpering. "It's Peggy, isn't it?"

Daisy nodded and bent down to check for a pulse. "She's dead. She's cold."

"I'll call 911."

"Why us?" Rose moaned. They were sitting on a bench in front of the post office while Tom Willis sealed off the building and parking lot. Emergency vehicles were pulling up. A crowd was growing across the street.

Daisy shrugged dejectedly. "Beats me. I feel like I'm wearing a 'Dead Bodies R Us' tee shirt. Need a dead body? We'll find you one. I mean, really, most people never find one dead body in their entire lives. We seem to attract them. And poor Malcolm. Look at him. It's not a pleasant thing for a little dog."

Malcolm was lying with his head on Daisy's feet staring blankly into space.

"It's not my idea of a good time either. And don't look now, but the good time just got worse."

Daisy looked down at the curb to see tall, incredibly handsome man getting out of an unmarked car and walking toward them. "Of course, it did. Thank God I took the time to put on make-up."

He nodded at Rose and said, "Daisy. We've got to stop meeting like this."

"For once we agree on something. I'd be ecstatic if we could stop meeting at all, ever."

Bill Greene, Daisy's rat-bastard, cheating, ex-husband, turned to Tom Willis and said, "What have we got here?"

"The woman who runs this place is lying near the door in the back. First glance, looks like blunt force trauma to the back of the head."

"All right. We need some crowd control and we'll have to block off the street."

Bill looked across the street and asked Rose, "Who's that?"

"Who's what? There must be fifty people there, Bill. Everybody and his Auntie Em have turned out to see what's up."

"The woman standing next to Angela. And what the hell has your mother got?"

Angela Forrest was standing on the sidewalk looking quite chic in an unwrinkled, white linen sheath draped with a blue silk scarf, and white strappy sandals. Daisy waved at her and said, "God help us! What is Mother holding? And, look, she brought Percy."

A tall, beautiful woman with short chestnut hair was standing next to Angela trying to dislodge Percy from her ankle.

Rose answered, "You mean Sally Henderson? She owns the flower shop. Why?"

"Just curious. I haven't seen her before."

Daisy smiled and chirped, "Looking around, Bill? Again? Not everything happy at home? Bambi getting a little too nuts for you?"

Bill started to say something just as Malcolm broke loose and darted out into the street causing an ambulance to slam on the brakes. He made it across and jumped onto Percy. The two started barking and running in circles around the crowd, trying to herd everyone into a tight group.

"Look, you two go home and I'll be there later. And take those moron dogs with you!" He turned to Tom and yelled, "And you, get all the rest of these idiots out of here!"

Bill was turning to go around to the back when he heard a woman scream. He looked past the crowd to see a man jogging across the bridge in a tee shirt and shorts with a baseball cap pulled low over his face.

"Hey! That guy's junk is hanging out of his pants."

As Bill watched, Angela pushed her way past Sally and a group of gawkers and headed after him. "And where's your mother going? This is turning into a freaking circus."

Daisy said, "Ooh, that's the Bostwick bobber. I've already told him his padiddle is less than appetizing, but I guess he didn't listen."

"For God's sake Daisy, you talked to that pervert?"

"Not so much talked as yelled at him as he ran by."

As Daisy was talking Tom pushed his way through the crowd and caught up with Angela, but by the time they made it to the bridge his quarry was gone.

Angela stamped her foot and said, "Drat, I missed him." She was pointing a large squirt gun in the direction the bobber had gone.

"Mrs. Forrest, please, don't try to catch this guy. He could be dangerous. Just leave it to me. I'll get him."

"Tom, for the hundredth time, call me Angela. I have no intention of catching him. I just wanted to get a good look."

"Huh?" Tom muttered and turned bright red.

"What's the matter? Oh! Oh for heaven's sake! His face. I wanted to see his face. Good Lord, certainly not his doo-watty. I want to be able to recognize him again if I see him in a crowd."

Tom shook his head. "Angela, I'm begging you, please let me take care of this."

Angela smiled. "You're such a worry-wart, Tom. Okay, he's all yours - for now."

They turned back and Angela joined Daisy and Rose in front of the post office. Tom walked over to the on-lookers and started shouting, "Okay, everybody go on home. Let our guys do their jobs."

Most of the crowd moved off slowly. Sally Henderson walked across the street and asked Rose, "What's going on? I heard someone's dead?"

Rose nodded. "Peggy. We found her in the parking lot."

"What happened?"

"I don't know. It could have been a heart attack."

"I guess the post office won't open today, will it?"

"Probably not. We're going home." She and Daisy grabbed Angela by the arm and trapped the dogs by stomping on their leashes as they ran by. "Okay guys, enough fun. You're making me crazy."

Crossing the bridge they met Abby and Brad walking over to see what the excitement was. Brad asked, "What's up?"

"I'm afraid the postmistress is dead," replied Rose.

"That sounds like a murder mystery, doesn't it? The Postmistress Is Dead," said Abby. "I guess I shouldn't joke. What happened to her? Do you know?"

Daisy sighed and said, "I don't know much. It could be a heart attack."

"Really? I didn't think she had one," Abby laughed. They gave her a look and Brad cringed and said, "It's not very funny, Abby."

"You're right. But I didn't even know her and nobody liked her from what I hear. It's just my way of dealing with unpleasant things."

"Well, we're going home and hiding for a while. You might as well go home, too. There's nothing to see and the police want us all out of the way."

They walked on, Angela in the lead with the dogs. Marc Proctor was standing on the porch when they got to the house. "Daisy, what's going on?"

"Oh you know, same old, same old. Another day, another body."

"Are you all right? Are you hurt?"

Daisy replied, "I'm fine. Peggy, not so much. Look Marc, Bill's coming by to get our statement in a little while. I'll tell you all about it afterward."

The ladies went upstairs and Angela went straight into the kitchen to brew tea. A few minutes later she carried a tray with a teapot and three mugs into the living room and set in on the coffee table.

Rose asked, "What's with the Super Soaker?"

Angela said, "It's for the 'bobber'. It shoots twenty-five feet. Would you believe it? I had a trainer tell me to use a water gun on Percy to discourage bad behavior. It hasn't done a lot for Percy. He actually seems to like it. But I thought it might work on our streaker."

"Mother, really, it's not a game. This guy could hurt you."

"That's what Tom said. Drink your tea."

Rose held the mug and said, "I have to say that even though that woman was a royal bitch, I am not happy she's dead. And I'm less happy that we found her. Anyone for something stronger than tea?"

Daisy said, "Well, it's barely ten o'clock, but, yeah, a little something wouldn't hurt."

Angela smiled and said, "I've already put some bourbon in the pot. A stress reliever. You girls have got to calm down. It was a heart attack. It could happen to anyone."

"No, it wasn't," said Rose. "I think she was beaten to death."

"Oh. I see. That's why Bill is here again?"

"Yes. I guess we just wait. Thank God for Tonya. She can open for us."

They were onto their second cup when the bell rang and Daisy went down to let Bill in.

"Okay, what in the Sam Hill were you doing at the post office at seven o'clock this morning?"

"And good morning to you, too," said Angela.

"Good morning. Now, what in the Sam Hill were you doing at the post office?"

Daisy ground her teeth and said, "Looking for dead bodies. We can never get enough of them."

Rose sighed and said, "We were taking a walk. I like to go before it gets too hot."

"And you were walking behind the post office because the parking lot is so scenic?"

While Daisy and Rose were waiting for the police to come they had decided to blame the whole thing on Malcolm. Rose looked at the little guy staring back at her and felt like a traitor, but said, "Of course not. Malcolm ran off. We followed him and found Peggy in the doorway."

Bill looked unconvinced, but asked, "Did you touch anything?"

"I felt for a pulse," said Daisy. "Then we just waited for you guys. What happened to her? Was she, you know, 'assaulted'?"

"No, doesn't look like it. It looks like she caught someone trying to break in and they hit her with something. It wasn't one of you, was it?"

Daisy drummed her fingers on the table and said, "Are you serious?"

"I have to ask. You found her. I understand that she and Rose had some sort of argument the other day."

"Everybody in the neighborhood had arguments with the woman. She was really quite unpleasant. And no. Neither of us killed her."

"Did you see anyone around this morning? Anything out of the ordinary?"

Rose sighed and said, "Just a dead body."

"You'll have to come in and sign statements. I'll have them ready for you."

"All right. And you might want to make a note that my name is Daisy Forrest, not Greene."

"You changed it? I thought you liked being Daisy Greene."

"No. You liked me being Daisy Greene. I didn't want to change my name at all, remember? But you got so snippy about it, I did."

"Well, Daisy, if I had known you felt that strongly about it, I would have let you hyphenate our last names."

"Daisy Forrest-Greene? That just sounds ridiculous. And clearly you weren't listening to me even then. I was so incredibly naïve. The whole name thing should have been a warning."

She paused for a moment, then stiffened and said, "And what the hell do you mean you'd have *let* me?"

"I didn't mean it like that. I just meant that I thought you liked being married and it hurts knowing you didn't even want my name."

"Hurts, does it? Hmm, just trying to remember which one of us didn't like being married. Oh, it was YOU! You really are such an incredible ass."

Bill was opening his mouth to respond, but Rose stepped in. "Stop! It's old news, water under the bridge, been there/done that. I could come up with a couple more clichés, but mostly I just don't want to hear it."

Bill ground his teeth a bit, got up and went to the door. "Okay, I'm out of here. Come to the station tomorrow morning and sign your official statements.

Angela had been pacing around the apartment with her squirt gun, listening. Just as Bill was turning to go, her hand jerked and she got him with the soaker. "Oops, sorry Bill. This thing's got a hairy trigger."

Bill automatically said, "Hair trigger!" and then looked down at the wet patch on the upper leg of his pants, glaring at her.

"Really, sorry. I just got this and I'm not very good yet. I really didn't mean to get your pants so wet. You have my sincerest apologies."

He glared a bit more, then turned and tramped down the steps.

Chapter Six

When they had stopped laughing Rose said, "Mother, you did that on purpose, didn't you? Not very nice."

Angela smiled serenely and said, "Well, neither is he. And, no, I did not do that on purpose. As I said I'm not very good with this, yet. I was aiming for his head."

Daisy smiled, "But you got his crotch. It was perfect! I really needed a good laugh. It's been a lousy day."

Rose yawned and said, "It certainly has." She looked at the clock on the desk. It's eleven and I'm hungry. How about an early lunch? Salad okay?"

Daisy replied, "Sounds great. I'll make the dressing."

Rose got up and went into the kitchen and started putting together a huge chef's salad. As she worked Rose asked, "Mother, why were you here so early this morning? I didn't even know you were coming by."

"Oh. I wanted to show you my squirt gun and tell you my plan for catching our little naked friend."

"Of course you did. Well, you are not going to catch our little naked friend. I mean it."

"I didn't mean 'catch'. I was just going to get him good and wet."

"Well, you're not!"

Angela narrowed her eyes and actually said, "Humph!" She turned to Daisy and said, "Okay. So who did it? Who killed Peggy and why? What's the scoop?"

Daisy looked at Rose. "Good question. There's a little more

to this than we told Bill. We weren't really chasing Malcolm this morning. He's just a good, little dog who took the rap for us."

She reached down and ruffled his head. Malcolm looked up at her from under his shaggy eyebrows and sniffed. "I swear he can understand everything we say."

They told Angela the whole story about Mattie and the blackmail and the mail going to the wrong places.

"We were going to try to find out who the P.O. Box next to ours belongs to."

"But why in heaven's name didn't you tell Bill all this. I know he's unpleasant…"

"And a liar and a cheat and a supercilious jerk," interrupted Daisy.

"Yes dear. He is all those things. But he is also a fairly competent policeman."

Rose said, "Because we want to keep Mattie out of all this, if it's possible. And we have no reason to think that Peggy was killed because of the blackmail business. It was probably just a break-in."

After lunch Angela went home and the sisters went down to the shop.

"It's been busy," said Tonya. "All sorts of people have been coming by hoping to find out what happened. What did happen, anyway? Tom stopped by for just a minute, but didn't say much. I think he was worried about me."

"Holy cow," said Rose, "Of course, he's worried about you. I've been so overwhelmed with finding Peggy's body, it didn't even dawn on me that there's a murderer on the loose. Again!"

Daisy told Tonya about finding the body and Bill investigating and the 'bobber' showing up. She didn't mention blackmail.

"Do you think that pervert could have done it? Maybe Peggy caught him and he killed her."

"If he did, he'd be pretty damned bold to run around the crime scene with his weezer hanging out and the police everywhere."

Rose said, "Not to mention Mother. If I were he, I'd be more afraid of her than the police. I don't know. I guess he could have done it."

"Well, what I do know," said Daisy, "is that we're back to extra precautions. All doors locked except the front. Tonya, if you're at all uncomfortable with someone in the shop, don't hesitate to use the panic button under the counter. I'd rather you embarrass a customer than become a victim."

Last fall, Daisy and Rose had a decent alarm system installed in the shop and apartment, but added a panic button in the shop after Daisy's close encounter with a certified knife-wielding nutcase. It rang at the police station, but also set off an ear-splitting alarm the whole neighborhood could hear.

"Oh, I will. And Tom did promise extra patrols. It's nice having our own policeman to look after us, isn't it?" said Tonya just as the bell over the door rang and a man walked in. He wasn't a customer. A small notebook and pencil were tucked into the pocket of his orange polo shirt and the belt of his light green slacks held a beeper, cell phone and what looked like a tape recorder.

"Jeff Moody, my favorite reporter," said Rose.

"Hi ladies."

Jeff Moody worked for the local newspaper, The Bostwick Bulletin. His beat was all of Bostwick and any news it had to offer. "I'm covering the murder and need to interview you."

"Ah. Well, we're not here right now and probably won't be for the foreseeable future. You know we can't say anything. Sorry."

"Look, help me out here, would ya? At least give me a quote for my story or my boss will have my butt."

Rose sighed and said, "No comment. There's your quote."

"Oh, come on. Were there any clues? Did you touch anything? This is the first real story I've had in a long time. You gotta help me out here."

"Sorry Jeff, but the police asked us not to talk about it yet. Call the police spokesman. He'll give you a story."

"I already have. I need a scoop. Will you at least promise to call me first if you decide to dish?"

Rose said, "Sure. But don't count on it anytime soon."

"Yeah, yeah. I know. Well, I'm outta here."

When he'd gone Daisy said, "That guy reminds me of someone."

"Who?"

"I don't know." Daisy thought a minute. "Maybe someone in the papers." She shook her head. "I'll think of it."

Several people had just come in and were looking around when Daisy stuck her head out of the office and motioned for Rose to join her. Rose mouthed, "What is it? We've got customers."

"Just come here for a minute."

"Tonya, I'll be right back." She walked back to the office and said, "Okay, what?"

"He could be the blackmailer."

"Who?

"Jeff Moody. Think about it. Nobody thinks anything of a reporter nosing around. He has access to all sorts of background information."

"Daisy, don't start."

"Start what?"

"You know good and well what. Every second person you see is going to be the blackmailer. Let it go for now. We've got work to do."

Daisy said, "Oh okay, I'm working. But we have to talk to Sally. And soon."

"We'll see her at the committee meeting tomorrow. We'll ask her to lunch."

"That should work. Speaking of the committee meeting, are we supposed to be doing anything in particular?"

"Yes we are." Rose reached into her desk drawer and handed a sheet of paper to her sister. "Here's the list. Have fun!"

Daisy and Rose were both on the Fourth of July committee. Old Towne liked to celebrate in a big, old-fashioned way. The streets were closed to traffic and the day started with a parade at nine in the morning.

Afterward, grills were fired up and the cooking started. The American Legion did a huge bull and oyster roast at the fire house. Many shops set up stalls with hot dogs, hamburgers, funnel cake, fresh strawberries and cream, and homemade ice cream.

In the afternoon the games started. An egg and spoon race, three legged race, bocce ball, a beautiful pet contest, and a taffy pull. At dusk a gorgeous fireworks display was set off at the golf course adjacent to the bike trail.

The committee met at the Tavern at ten the next morning. All ten members were there - Daisy, Rose, Brad Douglas, Sally Henderson, the Clovers, Michael Jenkins and his partner, Sam Lee, who ran the micro-brewery, Walt Miller, and Mary Newhart.

Walt Miller owned the bakery/deli and was the committee chairman. As he was going over the agenda for the Fourth, Daisy was busy scrutinizing everyone. She whispered in Rose's ear, "Rats! Nobody looks suspicious. Oh, but look at Brad. He looks really stressed. He's always so easy going, but you can see around his eyes. He looks anxious."

"Shut up and pay attention."

"And so does Mary. She's biting her nails."

Rose kicked Daisy's leg and hissed "Knock it off."

After the business was finished, Walt announced that the post office would be re-opening the next day. "I know that's a relief for all of us. But we need to talk about this murder and what kind of precautions to take. We really don't want people to be afraid to come to Old Towne."

"Does anyone know if the police have any leads?" asked Brad. They all looked toward Daisy and Rose.

"I have no idea," said Daisy. "If they do they haven't shared with me. I do know that Tom Willis said the police will be stepping up patrols. But I think we need to get the neighborhood watch active again."

Walt said, "I think so, too. I'll send an email out to all the shops this afternoon. I'll let them know about the police patrols and remind them of the Watch rules - see something suspicious, call a Watch member or 911." He looked directly at Daisy as he continued, "Never take action on your own. I guess that's it for now. See you all in two weeks for an update on preparation progress."

Daisy nudged Mary Newhart and said, "Why was he looking at me?"

Mary just laughed and said, "See ya."

On the way out Rose caught up with Sally and asked, "Sally, how about lunch? It's been a while. We need to catch up."

"Sounds good, but I can't today." She looked around distractedly and said, "Maybe Friday. I think I'm free."

"Friday's good. Are you all right? You look kind of, I don't know, anxious."

"I'm fine. Just busy. I'll see you Friday." She practically ran out the door.

As they were leaving, Jeff Moody jumped out of his car and blocked their way. "Look, please, I need some help here. The only thing going on lately is that stupid streaker. He's interesting enough, but I need a real story."

Rose said, "Sorry, Jeff, we really can't help you."

"Come on. You two solved that murder last year. I know you've got to be looking into who did this."

Daisy said, "Talk to Tom Willis. We don't know anything."

When they got back home Daisy said, "I really do think that Brad looked worried. And Mary did, too. She was biting her fingernails."

"Daisy, everybody's worried. Dead bodies at the post office don't inspire confidence, you know."

"Speaking of the post office. It reopens tomorrow."

"Yes. I heard Walt."

"Well, we still need to find out who rents Box 768."

"Daisy, you're insane if you think I'm going to break into the post office. I do not want to be the next one on some loony's hit list!"

A voice trilled, "Whose hit list?" Angela Forrest appeared in the doorway of the apartment, super-soaker in hand, Percy at her heels.

"The murderer's. I was just saying to Rose that since the post office reopens tomorrow, tonight might be our best chance to find out who rents that mailbox."

"Oh I see. Well, I think we should. We'll be fine. There are three of us after all. And I have my gun," she said patting the squirt gun fondly.

Rose threw up her hands and shouted, "You're both insane!"

Daisy said, "You know, I've never seen anyone throw up her hands. You read about people doing it, but I've never seen it. Looks a little nuts."

"I feel a little nuts!"

Angela said calmly, "Rose, dear, it's important to know who has that box. How about we just try to get in and if we can't do it easily, we come home. I've never picked a lock, but I've seen it done on TV all the time. How hard could it be?"

"Did you not hear Tom say that the police have stepped up patrols? And I'm guessing there's an alarm and probably cameras. So between the police and a murderer running around, you both still think this is a good idea?"

Daisy considered a moment. "Perhaps not a good idea, but a necessary one. I don't think there are any cameras or Bill would have been able to see the attack on Peggy. And if there's an alarm, we'll run.

"We really do need to find out who's been doing the blackmailing. And as mother said, if we can't get in and out quickly and quietly, we'll just come home. I won't even bring my tool kit." Daisy was referring to her 'essential toolkit for the modern covert operator' that she kept in an old Louis Vuitton knock-off for the odd break-in.

Rose sighed, "I'm going to jail. I just know it. And I have a dinner date with Peter on Saturday. I really don't think he's going to find a jailbird particularly attractive."

Daisy said, "Rose, we are not going to jail. I think we'll go at dawn!"

"Not dawn. People are up and moving at dawn. If we are really going to do this, we'll go at eleven. Everything's shut down by then."

Angela chirped, "Eleven it is. Well, I'm going home to take a nap and find some suitable attire!"

Chapter Seven

Angela walked in and Rose said, "Mother, what in God's name are you dressed for?"

"This is how I roll, honey. Ready for a little night-time action."

She was wearing a black cat suit, black ballet shoes and a black bandana covering her hair. And she was carrying her Super-Soaker.

Daisy said, "Mother really, a bit suspicious looking, isn't it? We all set?"

They put the dogs on their leashes and walked casually down the street and toward the park. As they were crossing the bridge a police cruiser pulled up next to them and Tom Willis rolled down his window.

"Everything okay?" He looked at Angela a little doubtfully.

"Just walking the dogs before bed," answered Daisy. "Everything quiet around here?"

"Seems to be." He hesitated a moment and then said, "Angela, you're not planning an attack on that streaker, are you?"

"Oh, heaven's no. Just letting Percy and Malcolm get a bit of air. It's so hot during the day that these poor little guys don't get enough exercise."

"Okay, ladies. Please, stay close to home and keep together. Don't forget there's a murderer out here somewhere."

Rose shivered, "How could we? We'll be careful. Good night."

Tom drove off slowly turning to go past the park and post office, then continued out toward the highway.

Daisy said, "Okay, we've probably got about half an hour before another patrol comes through. Let's move it!"

Everything seemed to be quiet. Only a couple of lights were on in some of the houses further down the street. They crossed in front of the post office and started up the alley to the back door. Malcolm and Percy stopped suddenly and started snarling and growling.

Rose said, "Okay, let's go home. The dogs don't like this."

But Angela was moving ahead, squirt gun in hand. "Come on girls," she whispered over her shoulder. As she got near to the corner of the building, they heard a door bang.

"Mother, stop!" Daisy hissed. Angela had reached the corner and stuck her head around when the sisters caught up with her.

Just as Rose whispered, "What do we do now?" a shadow ran from the back of the building toward them. Malcolm and Percy started pulling at their leashes and barking like crazy. The figure turned to his right and veered up the alley running all out toward the old neighborhood.

"What was that?" whispered Daisy.

"Someone else breaking into the post office?" answered Rose.

"Seems to be a popular pastime. Well, he's gone. We might as well take a look."

They sidled around the corner, the dogs trotting beside them. Malcolm was calm now, sniffing the area. Angela said, "You're right. Whoever it was is gone."

Daisy was inspecting the door. "Look. We don't even have to break in. The door's open!"

Rose had her phone out. "Daisy, are you nuts? We don't know the place is empty. We have to report this. That could have been the killer finishing the job Peggy interrupted."

"Just give me one minute, Rose. I'll just pop in and check out

60

the book. And then we'll call."

"He'll be long gone by then."

"He's probably long gone now."

While they were arguing, Angela had slipped into the door and was back. She was holding a red three-ring binder labeled 'POST OFFICE BOXES' with her bandana. "Is this what you wanted? I found it lying on the floor. The place is a mess."

"Mother! Put that back," cried Rose.

"Wait a second, Rose," said Daisy. "Just let me take a look."

She carefully turned the pages of the book by the edges. When she came to Box 768 she pulled out her cell phone and snapped a picture of the page. "One more second. All right, I've emailed it to myself."

Just then they saw headlights coming up the alley. Daisy handed the book to her mother and ran toward the car with the dogs in tow, as Rose pretended to dial 911 and Angela threw the book into the open door. They turned in time to see Tom Willis getting out of his car.

Daisy rushed up to him, "Thank God you're back. We were just calling the police. I think someone broke into the post office. The door's open and we saw someone running up the alley."

"Are you all right? What are you doing back here? You could have been killed. Go ahead and call 911. I'm going to see if I can find him."

Tom got back into his cruiser and drove up the alley. Rose made the emergency call.

Daisy said, "Rose, shout when you see Tom's car coming back."

Before Rose could respond Daisy, followed by Angela, had ducked into the doorway.

Rose looked at Malcolm and muttered, "They're both totally insane." Daisy stuck her head out the door and said, "I heard that!" then disappeared again.

A minute later Rose moved to the doorway and called softly, "Car lights. Get out of there now!"

Daisy and Angela slid out of the door and the three were standing in a row when Tom pulled up again. He got out of the cruiser and said, "I didn't see anyone. Did you get a good look? Can you describe him?"

Rose said, "No. It's so dark and he ran away from us. He was wearing a baggy black sweatshirt with the hood up, I think."

"Why were you back here, anyway?"

Rose answered, "The dogs started acting up when we got near the post office. Then they ran up the alley and sort of dragged us after them."

Tom took a quick look inside the building and around the doorway. Then he said, "You might as well go on home. This is going to take a while." He looked at Angela and frowned. "You didn't go in there by any chance, did you?"

Rose said, "Of course not. Do you think I'm crazy?"

"Just asking. Gotta cover all the bases."

"I know you do. Well, see you tomorrow, Tom."

They were walking back down the alley when an old Chevy S10 pulled up and Jeff Moody, hopped out.

"I heard the call out on the police band in my truck. So, what happened?"

"Ask Tom Willis. He's right back there."

"Oh come on, give me something. I had to write tomorrow's column without any help from you and my boss wasn't happy."

Daisy said, "There's nothing to tell. We were walking the dogs and they started barking and ran up the alley. It looks like someone broke into the post office."

Jeff looked at Angela and asked, "Why are you dressed like that?"

"Like what? You're very rude!" Angela wrinkled her nose and sniffed and said, "Come on Percy. Let's go home."

Rose threw herself onto the couch and said, "Whew! No more burgling for me. The strain is just too much."

"Oh come on, it wasn't that bad," said Daisy. She was pouring a lovely pink concoction into three tall, iced glasses. "Here, drink this. You'll feel better. And remember, we actually got what we went there for."

"And we didn't go to jail, dear, so you can have a nice date with Peter on Saturday," Angela chimed in. "I'm a little disappointed that I didn't get that man with my squirt gun, but he surprised me. I'll be ready for him next time."

Rose said emphatically, "No next time. There will be no next time."

Daisy rolled her eyes and said, "Oh, quit griping. We're all fine. Mother, that place was really trashed. Where did you find the book?"

"Just inside the door. The burglar must have dropped it when he heard the dogs."

Daisy patted Malcolm's head and said, "Good going, buddy."

Then she went to the desk, drink in hand, and turned on the computer. She brought up her Gmail account and said, "All righty then. Let's see who the blackmailing bully is who rents Box 768."

She opened her email and printed out the page from the record book. "Okay here it is - Charlie Taylor, 6201 Mill Street, Vienna, MD 21869. 555-228-2525. "Hmm. There are two IDs here, but they're illegible. That idiot Peggy – sorry, Peggy, but dead doesn't make you smart – must have set the copier set to darkest. This looks like a driver's license, but you can't see the picture or read anything. And I think the other ID is just a credit card. Not too much help. What do you think?"

Rose glanced over Daisy's shoulder, yawned and said, "That there's not much more we can do tonight, so I'm going to bed. We can figure it out in the morning."

Angela got up, too, and said, "Yes, I need to get out of this outfit. It's a little warmer than I thought it would be."

"Really? And I thought black spandex would be so comfy on a hot summer night."

"No need to be impertinent." Angela went upstairs and called down, "Good night girls. Are we walking in the morning?"

"Sure." Daisy turned off the computer and said, "We'll find out who this Charlie Taylor is tomorrow."

Daisy and Rose were climbing the stairs when Rose said, "Holy moly, I wonder if we just ran into Charlie Taylor."

"Ooh." Daisy stopped in mid-step. "Well, now I do too. Are all the doors locked?"

"Yes. And the alarm's on," answered Rose. She paused for a moment at the top of the stairs and said, "I think I'll just go down and put the bolt on the dog door."

Chapter Eight

It was past two in the morning. Rose had tossed and turned for over an hour listening for the sound of men in black hoodies breaking in. She had just fallen off to sleep when Roscoe jumped onto the bed and started kneading her hair like a deranged beautician.

"Go away, you idiot." She batted him away, but he came right back and started licking her face. "What is your problem?" She sat up and rubbed her eyes. "Oh, I locked you in, didn't I? Come on."

She slipped her feet into her old running shoes and padded out of her bedroom. She bumped into Daisy in the hall and yawned, "What is going on? Why are you up?"

Daisy said, "Malcolm needs to go out. Apparently, it's urgent."

Angela came out of her room and said, "So does Percy. He jumped onto my bed, sat on my shoulder, and then started – well, you know Percy. He's *never* done that before - at least, not to me."

"Then we'd better let them out."

All at once the three dumb chums started howling and hissing and generally acting as if someone had spiked their kibble. They bounded down the two flights of the rear steps, stopped short of the back door, and huddled together like refugees on a cold night.

"What is it with you guys?" asked Daisy as she got to the door. "Are you afraid of something, you crazy critters?"

And then Daisy and Rose looked out the window and saw the fire.

"Holy smoke, the dog house is on fire!" shouted Rose. She yanked open the door without thinking and the burglar alarm started keening. "Oh for gods sakes!" She turned to run back upstairs to the control pad just as Daisy rushed past her and out the door.

Rose entered the code and the noise stopped. She said, "Mother, stay here and answer the phone when the alarm people call."

She ran to the side of the house and grabbed a rake as Daisy pulled the garden hose around to the dog's igloo. Daisy sprayed water everywhere as Rose raked the embers out of the dog house and tamped down the ashes. They had it out in a couple of minutes.

Daisy kept watering, soaking everything she could reach, worried that something was still smoldering. Rose was checking the rest of the yard when she saw Mrs. Hudson standing on her porch in her hairpins, spindly legs peeking out from under her chartreuse chenille robe, and fuzzy, turquoise rabbits on her feet. She was an odd sight on an already very odd night.

She was hollering, "Is everything all right? I heard that awful alarm and then I saw the flames. What's going on?"

"Aunt Sarah, what are doing out here? What's all the noise?" Abby Wentworth shuffled onto the porch in a long tee shirt. She sniffed the acrid smoke and said, "Oh my God! What happened?"

Rose walked over to the fence. "Everything's okay. There was a small fire in the dog house."

"A fire? In the dog house? How did that happen?"

"I can't imagine. I know for a fact that neither of the dogs smokes."

Mrs. Hudson frowned and said angrily, "I don't see how you can laugh about a thing like this. The whole neighborhood could have gone up. You must have spilled some charcoal or something. You should be more careful. Really, you girls!"

She stomped back into the house muttering to herself. Abby shrugged, "Sorry about that. She's always been afraid of fire. How did it start?"

"I have no idea. Maybe it was kids smoking or something. I really don't know. We're just lucky the dogs and Roscoe woke us up. It's been so dry that if that walnut tree had caught, I hate to think what might have happened. What a night!"

A police car pulled up to the house and Rose sighed, "Good lord above, I just want to go to bed."

Tom Willis walked around the house as Daisy was putting the hose away. "What's going on? I was sitting over there at the post office waiting for someone to board up the door and I heard your alarm."

Rose said, "We had a fire in the dog house."

"It's out. Thank God it wasn't much. Come on in, Tom. I need a little relaxer," said Daisy.

They had just sat down in the living room and Tom had his notebook out when someone started pounding on the front door.

Daisy groaned, "Will this night never end?" and went down to answer it. She came back with Ron Tucker, their oldest neighbor in all senses of the word, in tow.

Mr. Tucker said, "Sorry to barge in, but I heard all the ruckus and wanted to make sure you gals were okay. Glad to see you here, Tom."

Angela came in from the kitchen with a tray of tall glasses filled with an orangey concoction. "Thank you, Ron. So sweet of you to check on us. A little fire in the dog house. No harm done. The girls and I are just having a little cocktail. Would you like one?"

Angela was standing there, tray in hand, in a flowing caftan looking like a hostess from the sixties. She had piled her blond curls on top of her head, brushed on some make-up and slipped about ten strands of beads around her neck.

Daisy and Rose looked at each other's damp hair and soot-stained faces.

Daisy whispered, "How does she do it? You and I look like refugees from an orphan's pajama party." Daisy was wearing an old red tank top and Joe Boxer sleep shorts. Rose had on a faded green nightshirt and her running shoes.

Rose whispered back, "Had I known I was going to be running around the yard and entertaining the neighborhood, I'd have worn my best jammies."

Ron Tucker said, "Oh, no thank you, Miss Angela. I'll be getting back. I need my beauty rest. Ha, ha! I'm just glad you're okay. Good night, all." Daisy walked him down to the front door.

A moment later as she was coming back up the stairs, she shouted, "Peter, what a surprise!"

Rose quickly made her way to the back staircase just as Peter Fleming walked into the living room with Daisy, trailed by Abby Wentworth now wearing a gauzy sundress.

He was saying, "I just wanted to see if everything is all right. I heard the alarm go off."

Angela stepped up with her tray and said, "How nice of you. Rose will be down in a minute. Abby, you're here too? My goodness, we've got quite a little party, don't we?"

"Care for a Fire Cracker? I was saving them for the Fourth, but this night has been a bit much."

"Thank you, Angela. That sounds good." She handed Peter a glass and he took a large sip. "Oh my God," he choked.

Angela smiled, "So glad you like it. That rum really does the trick."

Daisy tasted hers and croaked, "The Bacardi 151? Holy hell, Mother. How much did you put in?"

"A goodly splash. It's all on the top. Abby, what can I get you?"

Abby simpered. There was no other word for the coy look she was giving Peter. "Nothing, thank you, Mrs. Forrest. I'm afraid it might be too strong for me."

Angela beamed at her and whispered, "Nobody likes a goody-two-shoes, dear." She turned to Tom and said, "Yours is just orange juice. I know you're driving."

Tom smiled and said, "Thanks, Angela. Mr. Fleming, what are you doing here at this time of night, if you don't mind me asking?"

"Not at all. I've been taking inventory at the store. I want to open by July Fourth and need to have it finished."

Rose walked into the room wearing a clean magenta tee shirt, white shorts and sandals. She had brushed the ashes out of her hair and swiped on a bit of lip-gloss. She looked at the group and said, "Well, isn't this something? Peter. Abby. What are you doing here?"

Peter started to say something, but Abby jumped in with, "The fire upset me so much. I just knew I wouldn't be able to sleep. So when I saw your lights still on, I came on over." She tried the simpering damsel act on Tom Willis, but he ignored her. Then she turned to Peter again, but he was looking at Rose.

They all sat down and sipped their drinks. Daisy kept yawning. No one said much. Even Angela was having trouble staying bright. She wondered out loud, "I can't think how the igloo caught fire. Thank God the dogs were in the house tonight."

Percy jumped up on her lap and dozed off. Daisy looked at him enviously.

Peter put down his almost untouched glass, looked at his watch and stood up. "I didn't realize how late it is. I'm so glad you're all right, but I'd better be off. We're keeping you up."

Rose said, "Yes, I think it's time for bed. And you have quite a drive, Peter."

"Actually, I'm camping out at the shop."

Abby tittered. "I can't imagine you camping, Petey. Do you have a sleeping bag and a tent?"

He looked at her as he would at one of his more intellectually challenged students. "No. It's just an expression. I bought a daybed for the attic. I like working at night and it's easier this way. Rose, I'll see you Saturday. Good-night all. I can see myself out."

Abby jumped up, grabbed Peter's arm, and said, "Wait, Petey. I'd feel safer if you could walk me home."

Peter looked annoyed and Daisy said, "Of course you would. Good night Peter. Make sure she gets home in one piece."

Finally Tom found himself sitting alone with Daisy, Rose and Angela. He opened his notebook again and said, "Okay, ladies, what is going on? You just happen to find a body. You just happen to run into a burglar. And now you just happen to have a fire in the backyard."

Daisy and Rose looked at each other.

Rose said, "We don't know what's going on, Tom. But it wasn't an accident. Someone started that fire on purpose."

"Why do you say that?"

Daisy said, "Because whoever it was made a regular little camp fire in the dog house. You can see the remnants of the charcoal they used."

Rose said, "And I can't imagine why someone would do that. None of this makes sense."

Tom closed his notebook and stood up. "Okay. Well, it really is late, so I'll let you get back to sleep. I'll come by on my way home in the morning and take a look around the yard, if that's okay."

"Sure. Just don't wake me up. I think I could sleep for a week!" said Daisy. "Thanks, Tom – for keeping an eye on us."

Tom left. Angela, Daisy and Rose finished the Fire Crackers and trudged off to bed.

The smell of freshly brewed coffee woke Rose about nine. She stumbled into the kitchen followed slowly by Daisy to see her mother sitting at the table enjoying coffee cake and reading the paper.

Angela said, "I was just about to get you up. I'm so excited. We're in the paper!"

"What do you mean?"

"Look. Here we are on the front page. The three of us."

She held up the front page of the *Bostwick Bulletin.* Under the headline, 'Bostwick Postmistress Murdered' and a picture of the post office was a short article about the murder. But in the column on the right was a sidebar heading, 'Forrest Girls Find Body – Again!' and a picture of the three of them being escorted into the police station last December. Daisy grabbed the paper, "Jeff Moody is an absolute idiot! He did this on purpose because we wouldn't talk to him. Girls? Since when am I a girl? It's insulting."

Rose was reading over her shoulder and said, "That's what you're mad about? Look at the picture! Read the article! He makes it sound like we know all about the murder. And that picture makes us look like we committed it!"

"If the real murderer thinks we know all about him, we could be next on his hit list. I'd like to put Jeff Moody on that list."

"You know, I still think he might have done it. Anyone asinine enough to call us girls could easily kill someone. Well, what do we do now?"

Rose said, "We go to work. We've still got a business to run. We'll talk to Sally tomorrow and hope something turns up."

Angela said, "I'm going home. I've got an appointment with Lolita. She's going to read my aura and do my nails. And then, I think, a nap. This living on the edge is a bit tiring. Call me if you need me."

Chapter Nine

"We can pick up the mail after lunch with Sally. I assume the post office will be open today. It's driving me nuts that I haven't been able to get into our box for two days," said Rose as she and Daisy hiked back to their house early Friday morning from their routine walk.

"The mail? That's what's driving you crazy? Rose, we've got murderers, arsonists and streakers on the loose and you're worried about the mail?"

"Yes, I am. I love the mail. It's like opening Door Number Three. You don't know what you'll find - could be nothing or it could be a million dollars. It's the thrill of the unknown. Besides, I want to get a look at the new guy and see what damage the burglar did. Did you get anywhere with Charlie Taylor?"

Daisy sighed, "No. That phone number is to a pizza place. And a Leonard Wilkins apparently lives at that address with no phone number listed."

"So the whole break-in thing was pointless."

"Not really. We know that the blackmailer was looking for something, too."

Rose said, "We don't know if that guy was the blackmailer or the murderer or just some random burglar. Or if the blackmail and the murder are connected. Or if the murderer suddenly turned to arson for a change of pace. We don't *know* anything."

"Oh come on! All this stuff has to be connected. The thought of, what, four different bad guys running around Old Towne is nuts."

"Four?"

"Don't forget the streaker. I know he seems like comic relief, but he could be in this up to his doo-dads."

They had just dressed and were having a cup of tea in the sunroom when Tom Willis came by.

"Hi. I thought I'd check on you before I went off duty. Everything okay?"

Daisy smiled brightly. "We just saw our friendly neighborhood bobber!"

Tom ground his teeth. "I can't believe we can't catch this guy. Where was he?"

"Coming down Market toward the bike path. He saw us and ran like the wind toward the trees. He's quite speedy."

"At least your mother wasn't here. I'm afraid she's going to try to catch him. She could get hurt."

Rose said, "I know she's a little crazy, but I really think she just wants to use her new toy. She wouldn't get close to him. Mom's actually very sensible when it comes right down to it. And she's taken a self-defense course for women. She showed me some of the moves – how to grab privates and gouge eyeballs."

Tom shook his head. "I sure hope she'll never need to use them. I'd hate for anything to happen to her."

Daisy asked, "Did you find anything when you checked the yard yesterday?"

"Nope. No drug paraphernalia. No beer cans. I think you're right. It wasn't kids partying. Someone set that fire on purpose and I'd like to know why."

"Me, too. Things were creepy enough and now we can't even let the pets out at night."

Tom looked pointedly at Daisy and Rose. "Probably best if no one goes out at night. I'm going home now, but call me if anything else comes up."

Rose said, "We will. When are you off nights?"

"Now. I have forty-eight hours off and then I'm back on days."

"Tonya will be happy about that."

"I will, too. Not just because I miss seeing Tonya. Too much strange stuff happens on the nightshift. I'm ready to get back to boring."

At a quarter to one, Daisy, Rose and Sally Henderson were sitting in a booth munching onion rings.

Sally looked worse than the last time they had seen her. Her eyes were red and hair needed washing.

"Sally, you're not okay, are you?" Rose asked.

She started crying. "No, I'm not. I shouldn't have come. I'm not fit company right now."

Daisy held her hand and said, "It's all right. We think we know what's wrong and we want to help."

Sally sat up in her chair with a startled look. "You can't know. Oh my God, this is a nightmare."

Rose said, "You're being blackmailed, aren't you?"

She gasped, then nodded and the tears started flowing again.

Rose said, "Sally, you're not alone. There are other victims."

Sally wiped her eyes and said, "Others? You?"

"No. But we know of at least one more person."

"How did you know about me?"

Daisy said, "Really, we guessed. I mean, Rose and I know there's a blackmailer doing business in Old Towne and you seemed so distressed."

"Then you don't know why?"

"No. And we don't need to know."

Sally put her head in her hands and sighed, "I might as well tell you. It's bound to come out now. If I had just never tried to hide it, I'd probably be fine. But the whole thing snowballed and now I seem to be in this mess and I can't get out."

She took a deep breath, blew her nose and took a sip of her iced tea.

"When I was eighteen I was doing a semester at the University of Edinburgh. It was my first time away from home. I'd been a pretty wild teenager and I think my parents were hoping getting away would calm me down.

"But of course, it didn't. It was pretty intoxicating being completely on my own and I made some bad friends. I ended up getting arrested for possession of a small amount of marijuana and sentenced to a year in a Scottish jail."

Daisy said, "Wow!" and tried not to look as astonished as she felt.

"Wow is right. Well, that did it for me. I was so ashamed and embarrassed. I grew up really quickly, behaved myself in jail and was let out after six months. I came home, moved back to my parents' house, cleaned up my act and started a new life. When I applied for my small business loan, I lied and said I'd never been arrested. I guess no one checked back that far and I got the loan."

She sighed and looked out the window wistfully. Finally she said, "About five years ago I got a crank letter in the mail asking for twenty-five dollars. I just threw it out. I figured it was just one of those letters like the ones you get all the time in your email.

"But the next week another letter came. Same printing. This one said 'I know about Scotland. Leave $25 in a brown paper bag in the grey trash bin at the farmers market on Saturday morning'. I can't believe I was stupid enough to pay it, but I was afraid. I wasn't sure how much trouble I'd be in if the SBA found out I had lied. Not to mention how embarrassing the whole story would be. My fiancée doesn't know anything about it. My father doesn't even know!"

"What happened next?"

"Well, the letters kept coming every couple of months. But they never asked for much – twenty-five, fifty dollars.

"Then about two years ago the letters changed. They were typed, and they were nastier and were asking for a lot more money. I mean, they wanted five hundred or a thousand dollars at a time. And I had to mail it to this address in Vienna. I've been paying, but I can't keep it up. I don't know what I'm going to do." She looked at Daisy and Rose and said, "If he's not going after you, how did you find out about the blackmail?"

"We got an envelope of money in the mail by mistake. It seems this blackmailer is right here in Old Towne."

"Here? How do you know? I thought he must have moved since I had to mail the money now."

"Because the envelope we got was forwarded from Vienna," said Daisy. "You know how Peggy was really doing a number with the mail. Everybody was getting the wrong stuff and we ended up with an envelope full of money."

"And Peggy ended up dead!" said Sally. "Do you think she was the blackmailer?"

Daisy considered for a moment. "No. She wouldn't have put that envelope in our box."

"What do you think I should I do now? I'm sitting on pins and needles waiting for the next letter."

Rose said, "Let's see what Daisy and I can find out. In the meantime, you shouldn't send another cent to this guy. Tell the whole story to a lawyer. And your family."

"You're right. I should have done that in the first place. I know this sounds strange, but I'm glad you know. It's been so hard hiding it all."

They swung by the post office on the way home and got the mail out of their box. The place looked the same as always. But instead of an old lady reading a smutty romance behind the counter, an old man sat reading *You and Your Prostate*.

He smiled. "Hi. I'm Don Frazier. I'm sitting in until the powers-that-be decide who'll get this job permanently."

"I'm Rose Forrest and this is my sister, Daisy."

"You're the ladies who found her, aren't you?"

"We are, unfortunately." Rose was looking around the office. "Everything seems back to normal. You've been busy."

"It wasn't too bad. Had cleaners in yesterday. Then we had the alarm hooked up and fixed the security camera. Someone had disconnected it. Not to speak ill of the dead, but it seems like the lady who was killed wasn't too particular about things."

"She was getting old."

"I hear she was always a little off and pretty nasty to boot."

"She did have her moments. So you won't be here long?"

"No, ma'am. I'm due to retire in September. I was working in Greenbelt breaking in my replacement. But when that lady got herself killed, they figured I'd be of more use here."

"Well, it's nice to meet you. We've got to get going, but we'll probably be seeing you a lot."

As they were walking home, Daisy said, "He didn't seem too bothered about the murder and the break-in. I don't think I'd want to work there right now."

"Me neither. He also seemed like he might be a world-class gossip. That could be helpful. Well, what do we do next? I wish we could talk to Bill.

Daisy thought a minute. "I've got it! We could tell him that you were being blackmailed. We could make up something really sordid like an affair with a drug kingpin named Bubba Macintosh."

Rose said, "Bubba Macintosh? Really? He'd never believe that. No, we'll have to hold off until Mattie or Sally wants to go public."

Later that day as Rose was sitting at the dining room table going through three day's worth of mail she said, "Maybe we should talk to Mattie again and see how it went with Frank."

A moment later she blurted out, "Holy Bubba Macintosh! I

don't believe this."

"What?"

Rose held up a white cardboard photo envelope. "One last gift from Peggy. This was forwarded from Vienna and addressed to Occupant, Box 768."

She opened it and a baseball card slipped out.

"Mickey Mantle?" asked Daisy.

"You betcher! Autographed and dated April 17, 1953."

Daisy said, "Oh crap!"

"Exactly!"

"Are we sure it's Brad's card?"

"You think there are two of these hanging around? Besides there's a note with it."

"What's it say?"

Rose read, "This is it, you scum. I don't have anything else. But you gotta let me buy it back when I find the money.' It's not signed, of course, but it has to be from Brad."

Daisy said, "Fat chance of him buying it back. The blackmailer couldn't be that stupid." She thought a minute. "Unless Brad knows who the blackmailer is. How could we track down where this 'suite' is? If we made a trip to Vienna do you think we could find out?"

"No. Why would anyone tell us anything? We're nobody. We have to call Bill."

"Maybe we should talk to Brad before we call him."

"I don't think so. We don't know him like we know Mattie and Sally."

Daisy said, "Well, we don't know them as well as we thought, do we?"

"I guess not, but we don't know Brad at all, really. All we know is that he's good at getting rid of snakes. He could be violent. Think about it. He's willing to hand over a card that's worth two hundred thousand dollars. I'm guessing he has something really big to hide."

Daisy hesitated. "What should we do with the card in the meantime? And do we tell Bill about Mattie and Sally, too?"

Rose put the card on the table and thought a minute. "I'll hide the card in my sock drawer for now. And no, we won't tell him anything yet. We'll just give him the card and note and let him figure it out."

Chapter Ten

The late afternoon had been crazy. Everybody and his mother had come into the shop to chat, to ask what they were supposed to be doing for the Fourth, or to find out what was going on with the murder case.

It wasn't until after six that Daisy was able to turn the door sign to CLOSED. Rose came out of the office as Daisy was turning the lock and said, "I just got a chance to call to Bill. He said he'd come by around eight tonight."

"Okay. I know we need to let him in on this, but it really gripes my cookies."

"I know. So I thought that maybe I should talk to him alone. Your cookies would probably be a lot better-off."

Daisy laughed and said, "That they would. I wasn't going to be here anyway. Marc is taking me to Shakespeare in the Park at Montpelier Mansion. I have to hurry and change. We're going to dinner first."

"A real date! Are we getting serious?"

"No, I don't think that's ever going to happen. After last year's fiasco with the Maryland Fleur de Lis diamond, I don't think I could ever trust him completely. But he's fun and we have a good time together."

"Hmm. Well, I'm running over to Macy's before Bill gets here, so I won't see you until you get home."

"What do you need at Macy's on a Friday night?"

"I want to get something new to wear tomorrow night with Peter. I almost bought a dress the other day, but I need to try it on again to see if it really passes the 'twirling' test.

"What's the twirling test?"

"You know. You should never buy a piece of clothing unless it makes you want to twirl around in it. It works. I've saved a lot of money not buying clothes I'll never wear."

"Ah. Have fun twirling."

"You have fun, too, and say 'hi' to Marc for me."

Rose went out the back door and came right back in. "Have you seen my keys?" She was digging in her purse when Daisy waved them in the air a moment later and said, "You left them on the hall table."

"I did?" She shook her head. "I think I'm losing it. I don't remember going into the hall today at all. 'Bye again. Have fun tonight." She sat down quickly for luck, and then left.

Rose waved to Mrs. Hudson on her porch as she crossed the yard to the garage. Then she saw Malcolm sitting outside the ruins of his dog house.

She squatted beside him and said, "Oh, my poor baby. What nasty person did this to your house? We'll get you a new one on Monday. I promise. Now go inside and cool off, you hairy little fool."

Malcolm looked up at her with sad doggie eyes and wandered to the pet door and went in.

Mrs. Hudson chirped, "I believe that dog understands everything you say."

"I believe you're right, Mrs. H."

"Is there any news about that fire of yours?"

"No. It was probably kids with too much time on their hands."

"I expect so." She fanned herself with her hand and said, "I've got to get out of this heat. Good night." She turned and walked back inside.

It was nearly eight when Rose pulled the car into the

driveway. She ran up the front steps and started to put the key in the lock, but the door swung open.

She hesitated, then stepped into the foyer and called, "Daisy. Are you still here?"

Silence. She checked the alarm. Its red light was glowing. She stood there a minute and called, "Malcolm? Roscoe? Anybody home?"

Roscoe came running down the stairs and rubbed up against her ankles. She petted his head and said, "What's going on, little guy? Where is everybody? Daisy must not have pulled the door shut."

Rose closed the door and the alarm stayed armed, but silent. "Roscoe, did you break the alarm? It doesn't seem to be working." She picked the cat up and hesitantly started up the staircase with her Macy's bag in hand.

When she got to the top she paused again, then shook herself and said, "This is silly. Come on Roscoe, I'll get you a treat."

She left the bag in the living room and carried the cat into the kitchen. As she opened the refrigerator, she heard a noise from one of the bedrooms above her. She stood still, holding her breath.

"Probably Malcolm," she thought. But Roscoe hissed and jumped onto the counter, his hair standing on end. Then she definitely heard a floorboard creak.

The only way to get to the bedrooms was by a staircase that ran up the back of the house from the basement all the way to the attic. The front staircase was only one flight from the front door to the living room. So Rose grabbed the cat and whispered, "Okay Mr. R. I think we'd better get out of here," and started to tiptoeing to the front of the house.

She had reached the doorway the top of the front stairs when she heard footsteps behind her. The cat screamed and jumped from her arms. Rose tripped and felt something hard glance off the back of her head as she was falling onto the top step. She sensed someone stepping over her just before everything went black.

Rose woke up, but kept her eyes closed. Her head ached and she wondered how long she'd been out. She lay there trying to get her bearings when she felt strong arms wrap around her and lift her to her feet, pulling her into the living room. She started screaming and then did just what her mother taught her. She reached back and grabbed.

The arms that were holding her let go suddenly and she fell onto the couch.

Bill Greene grunted, then let out a moan.

Rose held her head, but managed to right herself. She looked up to see her ex-brother-in-law bent over, his hands covering his crotch.

"I'm so sorry. But, holy defensive tackle, it works!"

"What are you talking about?" croaked Bill.

"Mother's self-defense course. She told me how to escape if someone is pinning your arms. You kind of reach back and grab. Who knew?"

Bill stood up and glowered at her. "Yeah, well, you're right. It works. Are you all right? You were passed out at the top of the stairs. Did you trip?"

Rose rolled her head back and forth and said, "No. Well, yes, but then something hit me." She got up suddenly and ran to the door. "Did you see him leave?"

"I didn't see anyone at all. The front door was open. I came up and found you on the floor. What's going on Rose?"

Rose told him about coming home, finding the door open, hearing someone in the house, the cat jumping, and then tripping over her own feet.

"I think he hit me with something as I was falling."

"Okay, I'll take a look around. You stay here. By the way where is that dumb mutt of yours?"

"I don't know. He must be outside. I'm getting an icepack

and an aspirin. You want one?"

"No thanks. I'll be right back." Bill ran upstairs and came back a couple of minutes later. "You're right. Someone was up there."

Rose was now holding an icepack to her head. "Down here, too. They've been through everything in the office. How did they get in without setting the alarm off?"

Bill shrugged and said, "I don't know yet, but I'm calling this in. And then you can tell me why you called me in the first place."

Rose went upstairs while Bill made his call. Someone had been searching her room. The closet door was ajar and the dresser drawers were pulled open. She took her sock drawer out and dumped it onto the bed. The card was gone. She came back down shaking her head and said, "I can't believe this. That creep stole the baseball card."

Rose felt tears welling up in her eyes. She sniffed, straightened her shoulders and said, "I'm getting a drink. Can I get one for you?"

"Rose, you probably shouldn't have any alcohol. You could have a concussion."

Rose made herself a large vodka and tonic. As she squeezed fresh lime juice into it she said, "Well, I probably shouldn't have been hit on the head either."

She lifted her glass and said, "Here's mud in your eye! I never understood what that means."

"Me neither. Okay. What baseball card did the creep steal?" They sat together at the dining table, Rose holding the icepack to her head and sipping her drink. She told Bill about the fire in the dog house and running into the burglar at the post office and the mail getting all mixed up and finding the Mickey Mantle trading card in their mailbox with the note in it.

"I know it was Brad's card. He's had it hanging in his shop since it opened. He shows it to everybody. It sort of sounded like

84

he's being blackmailed. So Daisy and I figured we should tell you. You'd know what to do." Rose rested her head on the table and Roscoe perched beside her and purred into her ear.

"Where is Daisy?"

"Out for the evening. Well, what are you going to do about the baseball card?"

"Let me get this straight. You've been getting someone else's mail."

"Everybody has. That woman was really losing it. Maybe her eyes were going. She was mixing up everybody's mail. Malcolm even found an old tote bag filled with our mail lying in the bushes along the bike path." Rose looked around the room. "Where is Malcolm?"

"I asked you that before."

"Did you? Sorry, I'm not focusing very well. Let me go check his dog house. Only he doesn't have a dog house anymore. It burned down."

Bill face had turned to stone. He growled, "Okay, let's go look for him together before the tech guy gets here."

Rose looked at him. "Are you angry, Bill? I really am sorry about the grabbing thing."

"Rose, you could have been killed! I know we've had our differences, but you and Daisy still mean a lot to me. I want to find the bastard who did this."

"Oh. Okay. Me, too. Let's go find Malcolm."

They found the pitiful pooch behind the garage tied to a fence post. Someone had duct taped his muzzle and he was frantically pawing at it.

"Oh, Malcolm! Who did this to you?" cried Rose as she tried to pull the tape away. "I need scissors."

"Here." Bill held out a Swiss army knife. Rose took it and managed to get the duct tape off. She picked Malcolm up and carried him back inside.

She gently put Malcolm on the kitchen floor and got him a

treat.

She was mumbling to herself as she calmly got out the blender. "Taping my dog!" as she added ice. "Scaring me silly!" as she added rum and triple sec. "Beaning me on the head! I mean…" as she added frozen limeade and water. She smacked the lid onto the blender with such force Bill thought it might crack the glass. She turned on the blender and said, "This is just too much!" She poured the concoction into a pitcher.

Rose put the pitcher, glasses and a bowl for Malcolm on a tray and took it into the living room. She and the dog sat on the couch sipping while Roscoe perched on the table behind them.

"Rose, should the dog be drinking?"

Rose shrugged. "Why not? Life's short and then someone duct tapes you. He deserves a little pick-me-up."

They heard a car pull up in front of the house and Bill went down to the door. He came back followed by a harried looking man carrying a toolbox.

Bill said, "Start upstairs, Buzz. Rose, where did you have the card?"

"It was in the top drawer of my dresser. Under my socks."

"Okay. Start there, both bedrooms, and then do the desk down here. And make sure to get the duct tape on the front door."

Rose poured herself another glass and whimpered, "Tape on the door? What tape on the door?"

"Someone put brass-colored duct tape over the latch plate so it wouldn't lock. That's why the alarm didn't go off. The tape was thick enough that the door stayed shut, but the lock didn't engage. You wouldn't notice unless you really looked at it."

"Great!" There didn't seem much to say and they sat in silence for a few minutes. Finally, Buzz came downstairs, dusted the desk and said, "I'll get the door on my way out. And I'll need prints from the occupants for comparison and elimination."

Rose perked up. "We're already in your database. Just look

86

for Daisy and Rose. And Angela. She's in there too. We've all been finger-printed."

Bill said, "I'll get you the prints. Thanks for coming out on a Friday night."

"Sure. I'll let you know what I find out."

Buzz left and Bill said, "I'm going to talk to your neighbors to see if they saw anything. I'll make sure the door is locked. You stay here. And, Rose, you might want to go easy on the booze."

"Oh, I might. Then again…"

Bill left and Rose sat there rubbing Malcolm's head and wondering who could have been in the house. The frozen concoction was having its effect and her eyelids were heavy. Bill had only been gone a few minutes when she heard the front door open and soft footsteps on the stairs.

Chapter Eleven

Rose sat up and gently moved Malcolm to the end of the couch. She looked at him, put a finger over her lips and whispered, "Ssh!" Then she picked up the heavy wooden tray she'd carried the drinks on and quietly moved to the side of the hall doorway.

She was shaking as she raised the tray over her head, ready for the intruder. The footsteps stopped on the landing. Rose closed her eyes and threw her hands back to give some force to the blow. Unfortunately, she hit the door which bounced hard against the wall and smacked her in the head.

Rose dropped the tray and let out a yelp. "Ow, ow, ow, ow, ow. Boy that hurt!"

She opened her eyes when she heard Daisy shout, "Rose! What are you doing? You scared the life out of me."

"I scared you? Why were you creeping up the stairs? Oh, my head!" She plopped herself on the couch and put the ice pack back on.

"What? I wasn't creeping. I was just trying to be quiet. I saw Peter's car outside and thought you might be, hmm, you know. Why do you have an ice pack?"

"Peter's car is outside?" She squeezed her eyes tight and tried to focus. "Why are you home so early?"

"Marc wasn't feeling well. I told him not to order sushi in a Mexican restaurant, but boys will be idiots. Rose, are you all right? What the heck is going on?"

Rose poured a drink for each of them and told Daisy about

her night.

"Oh my God! I'll run you to the emergency room and they can check you out. You could have been killed...like Peggy."

"I'm all right. I am not going to a hospital. The headache was going away. Thank God I'm a klutz and was already falling when he hit me. But whacking myself with the door is an added bonus I could have done without."

"I guess we're both lucky, aren't we? You're lucky I wasn't the burglar. I'm lucky you are a klutz. You could have killed me."

"I know. Sorry. I just didn't want to get caught again."

"Well, next time keep your eyes open."

Daisy took a sip and sprawled on the sofa next to her sister. "This is getting totally out of hand. I mean, we had a burglar in our house! Did he take anything except the Mantle card?'

"I don't think so. I did a quick check. The jewelry in our boxes is still there. The TV, my iPad, and the silver are present and accounted for. Of course, I interrupted him. Maybe he just didn't get to anything else."

"Well, I think whoever it was broke in here to steal that baseball card. But who would even know we had it?"

She thought a moment, then smiled and said, "Wait, did you say you grabbed Bill's privates when he tried to help you up?"

Rose gasped, "Holy matzo balls, I did, didn't I? Ooo!"

"Well, bless your buttons. I hope you got him good."

"I think so. He yelled pretty loudly. But Daisy, he's actually been very decent tonight. So try to be civil. Are you hungry? I just realized I haven't eaten."

Daisy was just coming back from the kitchen with a plate filled with smoked Gouda, Genoa salami, sliced strawberries, and water crackers when they heard Bill at the front door. She went down to let him in.

As they came up the steps Bill said, "Daisy. I'm glad you're here. Do you think you can get Rose to go to the hospital?"

"I tried, but she says no. And I think she's okay. The headache's almost gone. She says you were very nice to her. Thanks."

"Helloooo," Rose trilled. "I'm right here. I can tell you about my head myself, thank you very much. It's okay. Really. And I add my thanks to Daisy's. Now, what did you find out? Did anyone see anything?"

"No. Nobody saw anything. Nobody heard anything. Everybody was at home enjoying their air conditioning. Ron Tucker did say his dog started acting up and woke him about seven-thirty."

"Woke him?"

"He nodded off watching Wheel of Fortune. Anyway he let the dog out, but says it started howling, so he brought it back in. I'm thinking that might be when Malcolm was tied up."

"Did you talk to Mrs. Hudson and Abby? And Peter?"

"I talked to Mrs. Hudson. She didn't notice anything. She ate and watched TV until I knocked on her door. She told me her niece was out for the evening. But I didn't see Fleming. The book store was dark. Why?"

"Daisy saw his car when she came home."

"Where?"

"Right across the street."

Bill looked out the front window and said, "Well, it's not there now." He opened his notepad and jotted something down. "All right. Who could have taped the door without being seen?"

"I guess anyone really," said Daisy. "The shop was open until six and things got a pretty busy this afternoon. The problem is we always keep that door locked. I don't see how anyone could have rigged it without the key."

Rose sat up. "I had to search for my keys when I ran out to Macy's this evening. I was sure I left them next to the register when we got back from lunch. But Daisy found them on the hall table. Somebody moved them."

"So you're saying that there was enough confusion this afternoon that someone could have picked up your keys, unlocked and taped the door, and tossed the keys on the table before he left without anyone noticing," said Bill. "Is that about right?"

"Yes. That's about right."

"And you think that someone was here specifically looking for this baseball card."

Rose nodded, then winced. "I guess so. Nothing else is missing."

"Are you sure?"

"Pretty sure. The jewelry in our bedrooms is just cheap stuff and it's all there. And the bathroom wasn't touched. The toothpaste was fine."

Bill looked at Daisy and said, "Maybe she should see a doctor."

Daisy laughed. "We keep our good pieces in a Crest box in the bathroom with the soap and stuff. This guy didn't even think to look there!"

"Or maybe I came home before he could get that far," said Rose.

Bill said, "Well, who was here this afternoon?"

"Let's see." Rose and Daisy thought back through the afternoon.

Rose said, "We didn't get back from lunch until about two-thirty. Tonya was here, of course. Mary came by to talk. That's not unusual."

Daisy chirped, "Marc dropped in to firm up plans for tonight. And Sally brought some flowers over."

Rose said, "Then Abby came by, looking for a gift for Mrs. Hudson. Brad dropped in for no discernible reason. I think he was hoping to run into Abby. Walt came in with the fireworks committee to talk about the Fourth."

"Who's on this committee?"

"Kelly and Anne Talbot. They own the Maryland Store. And Seth Morris, Morris Antiques. I mean it was Grand Central Station."

Rose added, "And we had a lot of customers. Even Peter came by to say hi and ask if I liked seafood."

Bill stood up and sighed, "So anyone could have rigged the door. But why would they? Who would have known you had this baseball card?"

Rose said, "I don't know."

"I'll look into this other PO Box and see if I can find out who owns it. And, tomorrow I'll make the rounds of the shops across the street and see if anyone saw anything at all. Right now, I think you'd better get some rest. I'm going to check your locks before I go. Make sure you set the alarm."

Rose stood and put a hand on Bill's arm. "Thanks, Bill."

Daisy stood, too, and said, "Yes, thank you. This does not mean that I have forgiven or forgotten anything."

"Understood. How was your date?"

"Oh, don't even go there. Not your business, in any way, shape or form!"

Bill said, "Fair enough. Good night."

Daisy followed him downstairs and watched as he checked all the doors and windows. Then she closed the door behind him, made sure it was locked and set the alarm.

Very early Saturday morning Daisy took Malcolm on a short walk through Old Towne. She had stuck her head in Rose's room to see if she wanted to come, but Rose grumbled that she hadn't fallen to sleep until after three and to leave her the hell alone. Oddly, Daisy had fallen asleep right away, slept soundly and had awakened before the alarm.

She sat in the little park and watched as Malcolm happily humped the truly hideous statue of a top-hatted penguin that welcomed one and all to Old Towne.

A car pulled to a stop in front of the penguin and Angela Forrest trilled, "Hop in, you two. I need to check on Rose."

Daisy got into the white Lexus RS and put Malcolm on her lap. Percy popped his head over the seat and yipped a happy good morning.

Daisy rubbed his head and said, "Mother, it's barely seven o'clock! And how do you know about Rose? Did Bill call you?"

"Bill? No. I had a dream that she needed me. You should have called me."

"A dream? Really? Well, everything's okay. Rose got a little bump on the head, but she's fine. I didn't call because it was late and there was nothing you could have done last night."

Angela parked the car in front of The Elms and looked at Daisy. "And how did she get a little bump?"

Daisy took a deep breath and told her mother about the evening.

"I see. Strangers are ransacking your home and beaning your sister. That is not good, not good at all." She held up a finger and continued, "On the plus side, Rose wasn't badly injured and Malcolm's okay. Undoubtedly, there are superior powers protecting you!" She patted the dog's head. "And how was your date?"

"A bit of a wash out. Marc got sick and brought me home early which turned out to be a good thing."

"You see! Superior powers at work!"

"She and Angela walked down the driveway with Malcolm and Percy in tow. When they got to the gate they both gasped in horror and Daisy shouted, "Roscoe!"

A bundle of orange fur was hanging from a noose draped over the lowest limb of a cherry tree next to the garage. Daisy sobbed as she ran to the tree and grabbed the cat. Then she screamed and threw it on the ground and thundered, "Someone around here is nuts!"

Malcolm and Percy bounded over to the furball and started

playing tug-o-war with it.

Angela cried, "Stop that. Put poor Roscoe down right now!" and then shrieked as poor Roscoe sauntered out of the pet door and into the yard to see what all the fuss was about.

Daisy clutched her mother's shoulder and said, "It's a stuffed animal, Mother. Some jackass wanted to scare us."

"Well, they did a fine job of it."

The door opened and Rose came out yawning. "What is all the commotion? I was really hoping for a quiet morning, but all hell seems to be breaking loose. What are those dogs doing? And, Mother, much as I love seeing you, what are you doing here?"

Daisy grabbed what was left of the stuffed cat from the dogs and said, "Inside you two. Come on, everyone. I need caffeine."

Angela picked up Roscoe and they all trooped up to the kitchen. Daisy threw the remains of Roscoe's effigy onto the table and told Rose how they had found it hanging in the tree.

Daisy made a pot of tea. Rose took an aspirin. Angela stroked Roscoe. They stared at each other in silence.

Finally Daisy said, "Okay ladies, time to figure out just what's going on here."

Chapter Twelve

The shop didn't open until noon on Saturdays so when Bill got there at ten-thirty, Rose was painting her nails, Daisy was at her computer, and Angela was baking, her go-to stress reliever.

Bill saw the furry, orange mess on the table and said, "Do I want to know?"

Daisy shook her head and said, "Probably not. But you should." She told him about finding the effigy.

"You know, everybody I've talked to looks perfectly sane. Well, almost everybody," he said as he glanced at Angela as she came out of the kitchen wearing a bright orange chef's toque and a neon green apron with a huge pink flamingo in rhinestone sunglasses saying, 'Bring on the cabana boys'.

"At any rate, none of your neighbors saw anyone take the keys or go in your front door. That girl Abby's a strange one. She kept staring at me and giggling. Then she started grabbing my arm and telling me how scared she is."

Daisy laughed, "We've seen her in action. She's annoying, but I don't think she bites."

A timer dinged in the kitchen and Angela went to turn it off. She came back a moment later with a plate of coffee cake and a pot of coffee.

Angela said, "Bill, sit. Have some cake and coffee."

Bill looked a little confused. "Thanks. It looks good. Not poisoned or anything, is it?"

"No. No poison. We're calling a truce until these mysteries are solved. We even put the dogs in the basement because you know what they say about dogs and policeman."

"What?"

Angela replied, "They make strange bedfellows. Without a doubt. Now, what can you tell us about the investigation into that woman's murder?"

"Angela, you know I can't talk about that, except to say it's an on-going investigation."

"For crying out loud, Bill," said Daisy, "we're not reporters. We live here and someone is trying to terrorize us. A woman's dead, Rose has been attacked and we can't let the pets out. Do you have a suspect or not?"

"No. No one that we feel strongly about. We haven't found the murder weapon. There are way too many prints at the post office to narrow anything down. So we're looking at motive and opportunity. Unfortunately, that list is growing. I even had to put you on it, Rose."

"What in God's name are you talking about, Bill?" shouted Daisy. "You know good and well Rose wouldn't kill anyone. She's non-violent. I mean she wouldn't even let me slash your tires or key your car."

Bill put his hands out in front of him. "Whoa. Daisy, I didn't say I think Rose killed her. I just had to put her on the list of the *many* people who had argued with Peggy Merritt.

"Who else is on the list?"

"A lot of people, but Peter Fleming was topping it. No alibi and it's a little too coincidental that this guy moves in here just when all this starts happening. But I couldn't find a real motive."

Rose and Daisy looked at each other and Daisy gave an imperceptible shake of her head.

Bill continued, "But now I've got Brad Douglas taking the top spot. After all, I understand that card could be worth nearly a quarter of a million dollars. Maybe he sends it to the blackmailer in a panic, but decides that was a really stupid thing to do. Maybe he thinks Peggy Merritt was the blackmailer and tries to get it back from her."

Rose said, "Or she just got in the way when he was breaking into the post office to steal it back from Box 768."

Daisy said, "I think it makes more sense that the blackmailer was looking for it. How would Brad know we might have it? And what about the rest of the crap that's been going on? The fire and the kitty-cat lynching?"

"I don't know if those incidents have anything to do with the murder. It seems unlikely. I'm going to talk to Brad Douglas right now. Keep your doors locked and the alarm on."

Angela picked up her squirt gun from the sideboard and said, "Not to worry. I'm planning on staying here until this villain is caught. If that so-and-so tries anything again, I'm ready for him."

Bill grimaced and said, "Right. Just make sure your doors are locked." He turned to leave, but paused for a moment as a stream of cold water ran down his back. He shook his head slightly, then just went on down the stairs.

Rose said, "Mother, put that thing away. We have a truce, remember."

"I know. It just goes off sometimes."

"Works for me," laughed Daisy. "Besides it's a hot day. He should thank you for cooling him off."

Rose checked her watch and said, "Time to open. Let's go Daisy. What are you doing this afternoon, Mother?"

"I think I'll take the dogs out for a bit of a walk. And Lenore Albert invited me for tea later on."

"Just be careful, please."

"Oh, I will. I've got the dogs and my gun. I'll be fine. What time is your big date?"

"Not a big date. Just dinner and he's picking me up at seven thirty."

"Good. I'll have some nibbles ready."

Daisy had been looking out the window at Peter's shop. "Are

you sure you'll be safe with him, Rose?"

"What do you mean? He's a little repressed, but I think deep down there's a nice guy waiting to get out."

"I'm thinking about what Bill said. What if Peter has something to do with the murder? Or the blackmail? Peggy was murdered after he got here."

"So? The blackmail started years ago - which is something we probably will have to tell Bill at some point."

"Well, Peter certainly knew the value of that baseball card. Maybe I should go with you."

"Me, too," chirped Angela. "We could double date!"

"Really? You don't think he'd find this a bit odd? I'll be fine. I've got my phone and my hairspray if I feel threatened. But I won't. So don't worry."

"I don't think hairspray really works all that well," said Daisy.

"It stings like crazy if you get it in your eyes. And makes your face all sticky. And pepper spray is illegal. Now, let's go to work."

At seven-fifteen Rose came into the living room wearing a sapphire blue, silk tank dress. She had pulled her auburn curls into an elegant chignon and wore a chunky gold necklace with matching earrings and bracelet.

Daisy looked up from the crossword puzzle she was working on and said, "Oh my! That's definitely a twirler."

"Not too much, is it?"

Angela walked in from the kitchen with a tray of hors d'oeuvre and said, "Absolutely not! You look lovely, dear. Where is he taking you?"

"I don't know. He said to dress for dinner. I hope we're not going too haute cuisine. Maybe I should eat something before we go."

Daisy said, "Oh just drink a lot. Everything tastes the same when you're a little looped."

"It doesn't really, you know. Besides, you're the one who said I need to keep my wits about me–just in case he's a lunatic head basher."

"You're right. Keep the old wits sharp. Have a glass of water and some salad. You'll have a grand time."

"In your ear, Daisy." Rose walked over to the window and looked out. Then she paced around the room looking at her watch. "This is silly. I'm actually a little nervous. What are you two going to do tonight?"

Daisy said, "Mother made a plan. We're going to the Tavern for dinner and then we're playing Scrabble while we watch the entire first and second seasons of *Downton Abbey*."

"Without me? Humph. Well, if you want something to read, Mother, I've got *Murder Gets a Life* on my night table. I know you like Anne George."

There was a quiet knock on the door. "That must be Peter." The knocking turned to pounding as Angela went down to let him in.

"Anxious, isn't he," commented Daisy.

Rose looked irritated. "Well, that's just annoying!"

Angela came back up trailed by Peter and Bill Greene. Daisy frowned and said, "Ah, I see. Bill, you never could just knock, could you?"

Bill looked at Daisy and said, "What?"

"Oh never mind. Peter, how are you? You look quite dashing." Peter was impressive in a blue blazer, striped tie and grey slacks.

Bill whispered under his breath, "All he needs is a straw hat and rowboat." Angela kicked him in the shin.

"Thank you, Daisy. Rose, you're lovely. Blue suits you."

"Thank you. Maybe we should go."

"Don't you have a few minutes for a cocktail and some shrimp?" asked Angela.

Bill was helping himself to the shrimp. "Yeah, you should try some. They're good."

"I'm afraid we can't stay. Our reservation is for eight-fifteen. Are you ready Rose?"

"I am." She picked up her purse and said, "See you later. Have fun with Scrabble."

They left and Bill said, "I don't like that guy. What do you know about him?"

"Bill, just why are you here?" asked Daisy. "You have nothing better to do on a Saturday evening?"

"Of course I do, but I wanted to tell you about my interview with Brad Douglas. I thought you'd want to know."

Angela said, "We certainly do. Sit down, Bill, and have some more shrimp. Can I get you a drink? I've made frozen Daiquiris."

"I'm sure Bill needs to be elsewhere, Mother."

Angela was pouring the slushy drink into cocktail glasses. "Daisy, we have a truce and we're civilized people. We can have a drinkie-poo together while Bill tells us what he's found out."

"No thanks, Angela. I'm driving."

"One little nip wouldn't hurt."

"Angela, I've had your cocktails."

"He's right, Mother. One drink and he'd be forced to stay here at least an hour. And we'd need to feed him. Truce or no truce, I'm not eating with him. Okay, what did Brad say? Did you mention us? Did you tell him we had the card? Did you accuse him of stealing it back?"

"No."

"No what?" asked Daisy.

"No to all that. I didn't want to give anything away at this point, so I just asked him again where he was when the Merritt woman was killed. He still maintains he was tucked up in bed alone like a good little Neanderthal. So I kept it conversational and asked where he was last night."

"Where was he?"

"Apparently umpiring a Babe Ruth game."

Daisy scowled, "Can he prove it?"

"We'll see. I'll talk to the coach. I also asked to see the baseball card. Said I'd heard a lot about it. He seemed uncomfortable, but he showed me a card in a frame."

Daisy said, "That had to be a fake card. I knew it looked different the other day. The color was wrong. Isn't there some way you can make him prove it's the original?"

"No. Meanwhile, I'm checking on his alibi before I go any further. I don't want him coming after you and Rose if he really has no idea where he sent it."

"Okay." Daisy reached for a shrimp only to find that Bill had eaten them all. "Well, thanks for the update. You can go now."

"I'm going. Bambi's waiting for me. She's dragging me to some country/western bar so we can line dance."

"Good for you! Y'all have fun now."

He gave her a look and said, "You all lock the doors and call me if anything turns up."

Daisy opened the door and shooed him out, "You bet. Now you just boot scoot on down the road now and leave us in peace."

Chapter Thirteen

At about nine Sunday morning, Daisy yawned and stretched, then rolled out of bed and shuffled to the bathroom. She looked in the mirror and grimaced, "Note to self: never let mother mix the cocktails again!"

She washed, brushed and took two ibuprofens. Then she slipped on her cotton robe and flip-flops and opened her door. The smell of fresh brewed coffee met her as she went into the hall. But she quickly drew back into her room when she saw Peter Fleming coming out of Rose's room moving toward the stairs.

She gave him a few minutes in which she herself put on a dab of lip gloss and blusher and changed into shorts and a tee. Then she went down to the kitchen. No one was there. She looked out the front window to see Peter driving off and Rose heading back into the house.

Rose came into the kitchen and Daisy smirked, "Good night?"

"Oh God, not really. You how sometimes life is trying to tell you not to bother. I think this is one of those times."

"I do know. That bad, huh?"

"It started okay. We went to The Ambrose Inn in Edgewater." The Ambrose Inn was a lovely mansion built in 1815 on a rise above the South River. It was originally home to Elias and Annabelle Ambrose. Since the death of the last Ambrose heir, it had gone through various incarnations and at present was a well-known four star restaurant.

"Oh, that's so beautiful!"

Angela came into the kitchen looking like she'd just spent a day at a spa. Daisy shook her head and said, "How do you do it? You had just as many daiquiris as I did."

Angela laughed and shrugged her shoulders. "I have no idea. Alcohol seems to have no effect on me."

Daisy chuckled and said, "Rose is telling me about her night. Peter just left."

Angela put her hands over her ears and said, "BWI!"

Rose asked, "BWI? What's BWI?"

"Too much information, of course."

"That's TMI, Mother."

"Is it? Then what's BWI?"

Daisy rolled her eyes and said, "Baltimore Washington Airport? Boating Writer's International? Boating While Intoxicated? Better With Ice cream? Could be anything, really."

"Oh, I guess you're right. Well then, not TMI, please."

Rose groaned, "There is no information to have too much of."

"They had just gotten to The Ambrose House when you came in."

Angela's eyes lit up. "The Ambrose House. How romantic!"

"It could have been. We were seated in a candlelit alcove looking out over the river. We had cocktails in the bar first and flirted a bit. He ordered a nice bottle of Pinot Blanc when we got to the table. But then he went all dominant male and tried to order for me. 'We'll start with the escargot, followed by the braised veal cheeks and eggplant."

Rose looked like she might be sick. "I mean really. Do you think he looked at that menu and said, 'What really revolting combination can I come up with to impress her?'

"So I very quietly said to the waiter, 'Perhaps you should come back in a few minutes" and he went off and Peter just stared at me."

"Then he said, 'I take it you don't want to try something new.

I thought you might want to broaden your horizons. The chef here is wonderful and now would be the time to experience fine cuisine.'

"And I said, 'I don't want to experience fine cuisine. I want something regular - a Cobb salad, shrimp cocktail and crab cakes with coleslaw.'

"He looked like he was going to cry, but I stood my ground. Then we had a lovely Bavarian with fresh berries for dessert and things started looking up. We took a drive along the waterfront in his beautiful car with the top down. He brought me home and I asked him to come up for coffee - by which I actually meant coffee, Mother. We were sitting on the couch when he bent over to pet Roscoe and his back went out. I mean he really couldn't move. He just sat there hunched over trying not to moan."

Angela said, "You should have gotten me up. I have some pills in my bag."

"I know. I took the liberty of going into that pharmacy you call your purse and got him a muscle relaxer and a couple of Advil. We waited for the muscle relaxer to start working and then I managed to get him up the stairs to my bedroom. I couldn't leave him on the couch in his condition. I got his shoes off and tucked him into bed."

Daisy said, "And did you tuck yourself in there, too?"

"No. Daisy, you are the soundest sleeper I know. I got in with you, but you didn't even notice. So that was my big date. As I said, I think the universe is telling me that Peter and I are not destined to be an item!"

"Not necessarily. Many couples get off to a rough start and end up happy," said Angela. "Your father and I had a few bumps at first, but it worked out very nicely."

"Mother, you caught him in bed with your real estate agent. That's not 'working out nicely.'"

"Oh, you know what I mean. We had some good years after a bumpy start. It is possible. However, that's all sailboats under the bridge. What are we doing today?"

Daisy went to the desk and got a pad of paper and pens. "Okay, ladies. Get your coffee or whatever. We're going to figure this whole mess out."

She handed them a pencil and paper and said, "Now, just like they do in mystery stories. We're going to brainstorm and list everything we can think of. What's first? I guess we start with the murder?"

Rose shook her head. "I think we need to go back further – to when the blackmail started five years ago."

Daisy nodded. "Right. We'll make a list of everything that's happened, starting with blackmail."

Half an hour later Rose looked at her sheet of paper and said, "Holy mysterious death, Batman, we've got quite a mess here. Here goes:

1. Five years ago Mattie Clover and Sally Henderson received extortion letters asking for small amounts of money - which they paid.

2. Mattie and Sally are being blackmailed because of mistakes they made when they were teenagers.

3. The letters changed two years ago. They got nastier and demanded a lot more money.

4. We find a payment from Mattie in our mailbox #769. A lot of mail is being misdirected.

5. Peggy Merritt is killed at the Post Office.

6. The Post Office is broken into and we manage to find out that Box 768 belongs to Charlie Taylor. We don't find anything on him.

7. We get Brad Douglas's Mickey Mantle baseball card in the mail. So we know he's being blackmailed, also. We think it must be about something serious.

8. Our dog house was set on fire and Roscoe was hanged in effigy.

9. Someone rigged our front door, broke in, beaned me,

and stole the baseball card."

Angela had been listening quietly, but now she sat up and said, "We can't forget the bobber. We may laugh, but it seems like he's always around and he's very bold."

"You're right. Ten on the list is the bobber." Rose added it to the bottom of the page.

"Now, first question: do we agree that there are two blackmailers? The original letters were much more benign, if you can say that about blackmail. More like someone needed some extra cash every now and then and tapped a likely source.

"But two years ago they turned really ugly. The tone changed, the method of payment changed and the amount demanded changed."

Daisy said, "The first guy might have needed a lot of money all of a sudden."

Rose said, "I don't think so. The second letters were a different personality. I think two blackmailers."

Daisy and Angela nodded, "Agreed. Two blackmailers."

Angela raised her hand, "Question. Or statement really. I think they must know each other. I can't believe that two separate blackmailers operate here in Old Towne and both choose Mattie and Sally as victims."

Rose said, "I'll add that with an asterisk. I think you're right, Mother. But it could be something else. Maybe the second blackmailer got a payment by mistake like we did. We got two of them!"

Daisy said, "Nope. That wouldn't work because the earlier payments weren't mailed."

"Rats! You're right. Okay. We assume they know each other. They could be working together…"

Angela jumped up excitedly, "Or Number One is being blackmailed by Number Two, Charlie Taylor."

"Exactly. Second question – how did the first blackmailer

know to blackmail Mattie and Sally? They aren't exactly obvious targets. Successful businesswomen, well-liked in town. Their current lives are squeaky clean."

Daisy answered, "I think that the original blackmailer must have known Mattie and Sally when they were teenagers. How else would anyone know what they had done twenty years ago?"

Angela said, "Anyone who lived in Old Towne might have heard gossip. It's a small town. There aren't many secrets. And twenty years ago it was smaller. That new development wasn't here."

"You're right, Mother. So we're looking for someone who's lived here for at least twenty years or so," said Daisy.

"Or someone who could easily get information from that time–like a reporter!" cried Angela.

"Jeff Moody? But he would only have been a little kid when Mattie and Sally were getting into trouble."

Rose had been pacing back and forth. She stopped and said, "And how would he know who to investigate? I can't think this blackmailer just pulled names out of a hat and looked into their background hoping for some good dirt.

"No. I'm afraid the original blackmailer is someone we all know. And I don't like the thought of that."

Daisy said, "Third question–did the blackmailer kill Peggy Merritt and/or break into the post office later?"

Angela raised her hand again.

Daisy said, "Yes, Ms. Forrest. What is it?"

"The fourth question. Why is someone trying to scare us silly by attacking our pets? And is this the same person who broke in here? And are they all this Charlie Taylor person? And where does Brad fit into all this? Is he just a victim?"

Rose said, "Well, that about sums everything up. We have the questions. Now what do we do about them?"

"Research." Daisy started making notes for a computer search. "I'm going to see what I can find out about Brad Douglas and this famous baseball card of his."

Rose added, "We need to talk to Mattie and Sally again and see if there was a connection back then. And try to convince them to talk to Bill."

"It's strange. Mattie and Sally both stopped paying, didn't they? And the blackmailer hasn't made anything public. I wonder why."

Rose thought a moment. "I think it's all gotten out of hand. I think this Charlie person did kill Peggy, probably by mistake, and now the whole thing is snowballing. I'll bet he just wants to get the baseball card and figure out a way to disappear without seeming obvious before the police figure it out."

Angela raised her hand again.

Daisy laughed. "Ms. Forrest?"

"I don't think the blackmailer is as worried about the police as he is about us. I think the fire and the thing with Roscoe are a warning to us to leave it alone."

"How would anyone know we're investigating?"

"That's simple, dear. The blackmailer knows that you got at least one blackmail payment by mistake. I don't know how he knows, but he came in search of the card, didn't he? And you two caught the last murderer we had here. Face it. Everyone knows we're snoops and that we have an in with the police."

"And, of course, if it was the blackmailer breaking into the post office, he knew we were there, too, didn't he?" said Rose.

"Okay. You're probably right. But the fire and the effigy thing just feel more childish. Like something the first blackmailer - we should call him something - would do."

Rose suggested "Let's call him what he is, a blackmailing little toad. BLT, for short."

Daisy chuckled, but then looked seriously at her sister and said, "Why do we keep saying 'him'?"

Rose hesitated a moment. "Why, indeed?"

Chapter Fourteen

Monday morning Rose was absently dusting the main counter. She said, "A quiet week. That's all I ask. No pranks, no break-ins, no police."

Daisy nodded, "That would be wonderful. Speaking of break-ins, did you ask Peter what his car was doing outside the other night?"

"I did. He said he had forgotten something at his shop and ran in to get it. He was only there a few minutes."

Daisy was teetering high on a ladder using a feather duster on the chandelier. "Did he say what 'something' he'd forgotten?"

"No. Why?" The ladder rocked a little. Rose screeched, "Careful, don't lean so much. You'll fall over."

"I'm fine. Just hold the bottom for me."

Rose grabbed the ladder and said, "What difference does it make what he was getting from the shop?"

"Because we really don't know if he was getting that something from his shop or from our house!"

"You honestly couldn't think it was Peter who hit me? I mean first, he wouldn't have been stupid enough to park right outside. And second, I just know it's not him."

"No. I don't really think it's Peter either. But I think we need to be careful." Daisy slowly backed down the ladder and Rose let go with a sigh of relief.

Daisy looked up at the chandelier and smiled. "I love the way it sparkles! Anyway, I'm going to call Mattie and Sally a little later and invite them for lunch next Sunday. I'll say we need to talk about the Fourth. That will give us the week to investigate a few things."

"Are you going to let them know they're both being blackmailed?"

"No. That would be betraying a trust. I think we should actually talk about the Fourth. We really do need to get a few things done soon. And if something interesting turns up in conversation, all the better!"

Rose turned to dust a framed picture hanging on the column behind the counter. She smiled as she looked at Aunt Lucy sitting on the front porch of The Elms. It was summer and Lucy was sipping a cup of tea.

Daisy looked over her shoulder at the picture and laughed, "You know there was no tea in that cup. It was bourbon with a couple of mint springs."

"Yes, it was, bless her little tea drinking heart! I guess that was one way of getting through the summer heat before air conditioning. But looking at this gives me an idea."

"What? Get them loaded?" asked Daisy.

"No. We just bring up Old Towne back in the day when Aunt Lucy was still around. See if there's a connection between Mattie and Sally. We might find out who they were friendly with, who their families were friendly with. Anyway, I thought if we got an idea of what the town was like when they were teenagers, we might be able to figure out who started blackmailing them."

"Sounds like a plan. But what about Brad? He doesn't seem to fit into the Old Towne picture."

"I know. I think we have to stick with looking for BLT1. If we can find him–or her–we'll also find number two."

"Do we include Mother?" asked Rose.

"We better. We have to keep her in the loop. I know we told Tom she wouldn't do anything stupid, but you're never sure with Mother. She may try to confront the bobber."

"What we really need to do is to get her to go home."

"Who's going home?" trilled Angela as she breezed in through the sunroom door with an armful of brightly colored flowers. "I do love your zinnias."

"Aren't they pretty? They're the only thing I seem to be able to grow in our one patch of sunlight," said Daisy. "Actually, Mother, we were hoping you'd consider going home. I know you want to take care of us, but you've put all of your own plans on hold to do it. And Rose and I are fine. I hate to think of you missing your poker club and mystery book club and edible garden club and mystical sessions with Lolita. You have a full plate without playing watchdog for us."

Angela looked downcast and sighed as she arranged the flowers in a beautiful crystal rose bowl. "If you don't want me, just say so."

Rose looked up to the heavens and said, "Of course we want you. It's just that I know we're keeping you from things you like to do and, as long as Daisy and I are together, we're safe enough."

Angela looked sheepish and said, "You think I might go after that nudie-man, don't you?"

Rose smiled, "It crossed our minds. How about this, you go home and do your regular things. If Daisy or I have to be here alone for any length of time, we'll call you."

"And we'll keep you up to date on any developments. We promise," added Daisy.

"Oh, all right. I was looking forward to our poker game tonight. We discovered a new game last week and it was so much fun. Seven card stud, red threes, all sevens and black nines wild and an extra down card dealt if you have a six or a two showing. I won a bundle."

"I'll bet you did. So that's settled. You go to your poker game and we'll call you if something comes up."

Angela gave each of her girls a hug and said, "You know I

worry. Did you call the alarm people?"

Rose said, "First thing this morning. They're coming out tomorrow to see what they can do to prevent the same thing happening again."

"Good. Well, if you really don't need me right now, I'll be off. I like to take a little nap before our game. Oh, I did borrow your Ann George mystery the other night. I'm taking it with me." Angela went off to gather up Percy and her bag.

Daisy chuckled, "How can they possibly figure out who wins?"

Later that afternoon, Daisy sat down at the computer to begin her search into Brad's background.

Rose said, "What are you looking for exactly?"

"Anything I can find." Fifteen minutes later she said, "Look at this." She hit print, then pulled a sheet from the printer and handed Rose an article from The Washington Post dated April 18, 1953.

Next to the story headlined 'Mantle's 565 foot Home Run Clears Left Field Stands' was a picture of a little kid holding a baseball card. The caption read, "Nine year old Bobby Lee Dove and his autographed Mantle rookie card. 'Mr. Mantle was really nice and signed my card on my birthday. He even said he'd try to hit one out for me,' said Bobby. And, boy, did the Mick come through!"

"So this must be Brad's father. But they don't have the same last name."

"Maybe his mother remarried or something. Let's Google Bobby Lee Dove and see what we can find."

After another half hour of searching with Rose looking over her shoulder, Daisy had found a reference to the picture in the Post and a death notice.

"Here he is. Bobby Lee Dove died November 12, 1996. It says he was survived by his wife of twenty-two years, Elyse

Dove, his son Carl Lee, and his daughter, Margaret Ann. No mention of a son named Brad. Maybe this isn't the same card. Maybe Brad's father had another one."

Rose said, "Oh come on, that's crazy; two kids, same April 17th birthday, same story about asking Mantle to hit a home run for him. No, this has to be Brad's card. Where did Bobby Lee live?" asked Rose.

"The same place Dad grew up - Fredericksburg, Virginia."

"Hmm. I wonder if Elyse still lives there."

"Let's see." Daisy brought up the White Pages and found six Doves living in Fredericksburg. "There's only one E. Dove, age sixty-two. That could be his wife." She wrote the address and phone number down. "No Margaret or Carl."

"Margaret Dove? That sounds familiar for some reason," said Rose. "Check and see if Google has anything to say about Margaret."

Daisy typed in a few lines, got a hit in The Washington Post, read for a minute and said, "Oh my God. Of course the name sounds familiar. Margaret Dove disappeared in 2008 when she was on vacation with friends on the Outer Banks of North Carolina. We were down there the week after it happened. The whole island was still looking for her."

"That's right. Posters were up everywhere. Did they ever find her? I don't remember."

Daisy thought a minute and said, "This article doesn't say much other than she's a missing girl from Virginia."

Rose said, "The Outer Banks? That's a coincidence."

"What is?"

"Brad goes to a big card show on the Outer Banks every year. I really want to know how he got that card."

"Me, too. And I'd like to find out more about Elyse Dove's disappearance. I wonder if Tom Willis has any contacts down there. I'm calling him." Tom was out, so Daisy left a message. "Well, that's all I can do for now. We should probably tell Bill about this."

"Yes. We should," answered Rose.

"But then again, if I can find this stuff on Google, so can he. I mean he has all the resources of the state police at his disposal. So, I say tough cookies if he hasn't got the brains to look."

Rose thought a moment. "I'll agree for right now. But I'm telling him if we find out anything concrete linking Brad to this Margaret Dove or her family. And I'm guessing there is a link, and that the blackmailer knows what it is."

"What! You think Brad murdered her?"

"No. Not really. I don't know. I have no idea. I just figure that if the baseball card belonged to this Bobby Lee Dove and now Brad has it, he must have gotten it from one of the Doves somehow. And if he had gotten it legitimately, he wouldn't be telling the family heirloom story."

Daisy was chewing her thumbnail. "I wonder if Elyse Dove would talk to us."

Rose answered, "Maybe we could call her later, but let's see what Tom can find out first."

Tom got back to Daisy Monday night. As it happened a friend of his from the police academy worked down there. It took a little persuading on her part, but Daisy managed to convince him to make the call.

"Just why do you want to know about this girl?"

"Basically, I'm just being nosy. Rose and I were there on vacation the week after she disappeared. I want to see if they ever found her. You know how the news drops the story when it gets old."

"Daisy, I think you're up to something."

"Me? Not up to anything. I'm just curious. It was a big deal."

Tom laughed, "Well, this seems harmless enough. I'll give Mike a call and see what I can find out. But, if this has anything to do with what's been going on around here – although I can't see how it would – you had better tell me."

"Absolutely! If there's anything to tell, you'll be the first to know."

Daisy could picture Tom shaking his head. He just said, "Why don't I believe that?" and hung up.

Rose's wish for a quiet week lasted all the way until Wednesday. For two whole days no fires lit up the night, no one got hit on the head, no unsightly body parts were being displayed.

But Wednesday morning when she let the pets out onto the back porch, she stepped onto a sopping wet doormat. Water was everywhere. Someone had turned the garden hose on full force and left it running. Rose ran to the spigot and turned the water off, then came back and called upstairs, "Daisy, come here. Hurry!"

Daisy bounded down the stairs and out the door, stepped onto the wet mat, and yelped, "Dammit, I just bought these sandals. Where did all this water come from?"

"Someone turned the hose on. Look at the scratch marks on the dog door. I think they were trying to flood the house!"

Daisy looked at the door and said, "You're right. It looks like someone was trying to wedge the hose under the flap. Thank God we've been locking it at night. It could have been a real nightmare. It's bad enough as it is. Look at this mess!"

The porch was scattered with soaking wet deck-furniture cushions. Normally they were kept stacked in a storage closet on the porch next to the back door. But the closet door had been wrenched off its hinges and the cushions had been laid out end to end and soaked through.

The small zinnia bed next to the little patio had been totally drowned and the flowers had been pulled up and tossed over the yard.

"What in blue blazes is going on?" cried Rose. "Who does

this sort of thing? Who in his right mind goes after defenseless zinnias for crying out loud?"

"Beats me. Who in her right mind says 'blue blazes'?" said Daisy as she took off her sandals and put them in the sun. "Let's get these cushions out on the patio so they can dry. We'll have to get new ones if they get moldy."

She stood looking at the chaos around her and said, "You know what? This is getting really old. If I find the little fiend who's doing this, I might just ram that hose right up his..."

Rose cut her off, "Daisy!"

"I was going to say nose."

Rose bent over to pick up the wet door mat. A piece of bluish fuzz was stuck under a nail in the decking. She picked it up, studied it for a minute, and showed it to Daisy. "What do you think this is?"

"I don't know. Where was it?" asked Daisy as she took the fiber and looked at it in the sunshine.

"Caught on a nail under the welcome mat."

"It could just be part of Malcolm's chew-baby."

"Chew-baby's not blue."

"Then it's probably lint from the drier vent."

"I don't think so. I think this is our first real clue. Even though I don't know exactly what it is."

"Okay Nancy Drew, it's a clue. Now let's clean this mess up."

Chapter Fifteen

"Aaaaaaaaaaa! I do not believe this!" Daisy was standing at the kitchen table in her nightshirt, Thursday's Bostwick Bulletin clenched in her hands. "He's done it again, that little worm."

Rose walked into the kitchen carrying a load of laundry. "What?"

Daisy shoved the paper at Rose so hard she knocked the laundry basket out of Rose's hands. "Daisy, calm down and pick up my nightgown." Rose studied the paper for a moment and said resignedly, "Well, Mother's going to love it."

There on the front page was Angela Forrest in her cat woman suit. She appeared to be staring raptly at the picture in the adjacent column which was a blurry photo of, according to the caption, the 'bobber' running away from the camera. There was no way of knowing who it was, of course. A man jogging in shorts and a tee shirt in the middle of summer was hardly extraordinary.

Two stories accompanied the pictures: One, the tale of Roscoe being hanged in effigy and the on-going crime spree in Old Towne; the other, the elusive streaker that was ruining 'the peace of our little town' to use the reporter's words.

Daisy groused, "It makes Mother look like a lascivious lunatic. And the story draws everybody's attention right back to us! And where did he get the story? We didn't tell anyone but Bill about Roscoe."

Rose put the paper down and gathered her laundry and said, "I think that reporter lurks."

"He does, doesn't he? He always seems to be there, taking pictures and poking his nose where it doesn't belong. I think that's more than coincidence."

They heard a knocking at the front door and Rose said, "What now? I just want to do a load of wash. Is that too much to ask?"

She put the basket down again and tramped off to the front of the house. Daisy heard two sets of footsteps coming back up the stairs and thought, "Mother forgot her key."

But it wasn't Angela. It was Peter Fleming. Rose muttered something to Peter and hurried to the back stairs and up to her room.

Daisy quickly pulled down her nightshirt to cover as much as possible and said, "Peter! What a surprise. Just give me a minute and I'll get you some coffee." Then she hastily joined her sister.

Rose was fuming. "What kind of deranged mind thinks it's appropriate to drop in on people at the crack of dawn? Who does this?"

She was quickly washing her face and swiping on a bit of make up while Daisy changed into shorts and a top.

"Apparently Peter's deranged mind thinks it's just ducky."

"Well, he's nuts. Can I borrow your yellow blouse? All my tops are in the laundry basket."

"Sure."

"Okay, how do I look? I need to wash my hair."

Daisy looked her sister over and said, "You're fine. It's eight o'clock in the morning, he can't expect much. Besides the last time you saw him, he was bent over like a pretzel."

Daisy brightened, "Look at it like this. You won't have to worry about those first awkward mornings after you sleep together. You know, when you sneak out of bed to brush your teeth and put your make-up on before he's up, so he'll think you always wake up dewy-eyed and minty fresh. You've already seen each other at your crummiest."

"Probably guaranteeing there won't be any sleepovers."

Peter was holding the paper and looking out the window when they came back down. "Why are all of your cushions lying out on the patio?"

"Our little prankster was out again the other night."

"The one they wrote about in today's paper?"

Rose said, "That's the one. At least it had better be. I really hope there's only one stinker out there trying to drive us crazy. He tried to flood our basement, but couldn't. So he just soaked anything he could find."

"Your mother looks rather odd," said Peter.

Rose bristled a little. "She likes to dress for the occasion."

"And for what occasion might she be dressing in that?"

Daisy looked at Rose. "Actually, we were walking the dogs. Peter, you seem to be on a high-ish sort of horse this morning. Come down and just enjoy my mother's eccentricities, like we do."

"I'm sorry you think so. I must say I just don't understand people most of the time."

Daisy shook her head. "No, you really don't, do you? And yet you teach philosophy. Oh well, mystery is the spice of life!"

Rose added, "Not that we're not pleased to see you, but what are you doing here at this hour?"

"Oh, ah. Actually, I was hoping for a cup of coffee. I spent the last few nights at the bookstore. When I got up this morning I found that I'd run out. And I wanted to thank you for the other night."

Rose looked at him for a moment, smiled and said, "Sure, you can have a cup of coffee. And you're welcome. Actually, I should be thanking you. It was a lovely evening for the most part."

Daisy was getting a little tired of this weird off-and-on flirtation. She said, "How's your back? And how come you've been sleeping at the shop?"

"It's better, thank you."

"Because sleeping on a cot in the attic probably isn't the best thing for a bad back."

"No, it's probably not. But I want to get the place in order so I can open by the Fourth. And the only time I have is at night."

Daisy handed Peter a cup of coffee. "So you were here Wednesday night?"

"Yes, I was."

"Were you up late? Did you happen to notice anyone hanging around our house?" asked Rose.

"No. I was busy cataloging. I didn't see anyone."

"Rats! I'd really like to catch this guy."

"Do you have any idea who would do these sorts of things?" asked Peter. "This sounds a bit dramatic, but do you have any enemies?"

Rose thought a moment and said, "I really don't think we do. I guess I'm a little afraid it's the same person who broke in here. Or that it might be related to the murder."

"But why would it be? Do you know anything about that woman's murder?"

Daisy said, "Nothing at all. We just found her."

"But everybody says that you and Rose solved that murder last year. Maybe the killer is afraid you're investigating this one and wants to put you off the idea."

Rose started to answer him, but caught a look from Daisy, so she just said, "I hardly think so. The killer last year sort of landed in our laps. We don't investigate things. We simply run a gift shop."

Daisy chimed in, "Speaking of which, we'd better get a move on. We open at ten."

Peter stood and said, "Of course. I'll be going. Thank you for the coffee."

Rose walked him to the door. He gave her a kiss on the cheek and said, "I would like to see you again."

She smiled, "That would be nice. Maybe next weekend."

"I'll be in touch."

Rose shook her head as she watched him walk across the street. She was turning to go back into the house when she noticed a familiar figure in a baseball cap, red shorts and a tee shirt jogging toward her.

She yelled up the steps, "Daisy, come out here. The pervert's back!"

Daisy came running down the steps in time to see Rose step onto the sidewalk and block his way. She launched into a tirade yelling at him to cover himself up for crying out loud. Asking what kind of pervert was he, anyway, and telling him to wait right there, she was calling the police.

Daisy quickly shook her shoulder and said in a low voice, "It's not him."

"What!" yelled Rose.

"It's not him. He's completely covered, Rose. Nothing hanging out. Wrong hat. No sunglasses."

Rose looked down, then up, and said, "Oh my lord in Cincinnati, I am so sorry. I thought you were someone else."

The poor sap looked horrified as he backed away from Rose and Daisy. He shouted, "You're a lunatic," as he turned and ran back the way he came.

Rose and Daisy got back into the house and Daisy burst out laughing. "That man must think you're completely insane. What were you doing, Rose?"

Rose said, "Look, I've had it this morning. First, that idiotic article in the newspaper. Then Peter just dropping in and being, you know, Peter! All I wanted to do was wash my underwear. When I saw that guy jogging down the street, I just lost it. And how do you know he isn't the bobber? He could have been and he just wasn't airing out the old ding-dong this morning."

"I don't think so. Every time he's been seen, the bobber's been wearing a John Deere hat and sunglasses. Why would he change? And he never gets close enough to anyone to get caught.

No, you just made an ass out of yourself in front of a totally innocent stranger."

"Shove it, Daisy. I don't need this this morning. I'm doing my laundry." She picked up her basket and stomped down the stairs.

She stomped back up the stairs in less than a minute. She put the basket down and demanded, "Hey, what was with the smoke signals when we were talking to Peter?"

"Um, nothing really. I just don't think you should tell him too much. I don't know if we can trust him."

"What do you mean?"

"Well, what do we really know about Peter Fleming? Only that he's a good looking, wealthy, book store owner with a bad back and peculiar taste in food. Think about it. He's been at his shop each time something's happened. He was there the night of the fire. His car was outside the night you were attacked. And now we find out that he was there Wednesday night, too. And all of this started happening after he bought the bookstore. I just don't think we know him all that well. I mean, what the heck is he doing in that shop all night long?"

"Taking inventory and cataloging. That can take a long time," answered Rose.

"I don't think so. Hazel kept great records and she stocked the shelves like a library. A place for every book and every book in its place." Hazel Monroe was the previous owner of the Book Renew. "And why is he sleeping there when he's got a beautiful home of his own?"

"I know those are all good questions, Daisy. But I can't believe Peter is responsible for the pranks. He's not like that. The pranks are childish. And Peter is anything, but childish. And I am sure he did not attack me. But now you've made me wonder why he spends so many nights there." Rose shook her head. "I wish you hadn't said anything. You've got me doubting him. And I think I'm getting to like him a little. At least, when he's not being a jerk."

"I know. And he's probably a really nice man." Daisy smiled and added, "You know what we could do?"

"No, we couldn't," Rose said in a steely voice.

"Sure we could. We just try to find out what he's doing there at night. We wouldn't even have to break in, just look in the window. A little peeping never hurt anyone. Think about it."

"I don't need to think about it. He and I are going out again next weekend. I'll just ask him why he's there all the time."

Daisy demanded, "And what if the answer is he's a blackmailing S.O.B. who killed Peggy Merritt and whacked you over the head? I don't think you should go out again until we know more about him."

"More about whom?" asked Angela Forrest as she entered the kitchen.

Both women jumped and Rose yelped, "Mother, why are you sneaking up on us?"

"I wasn't sneaking. I can't help it if I'm a quiet walker. I yoo-hooed in the stairwell, but I guess you didn't hear me." She looked down at the paper on the table and said, "Oh my, that's unfortunate. I appear to be leering at that man. Who is he?"

"He's supposed to be the bobber."

"Well, he's not! Bob the Knob is thinner. And that man has a tattoo on his leg. Old Bob doesn't."

She studied the picture for a moment and said, "It looks like a giant spider, doesn't it? I wonder why people get tattoos. I've never really understood it. And it's not because I'm older. I didn't like them when I was young, either"

"My only tattoo question is how you know the bobber doesn't have one," Daisy said.

"Oh, I got a good look at him as he ran across the bridge the day the post office woman was killed. Remember, Tom and I tried to catch him. We didn't, of course. But I clearly saw his back and there was no tattoo on his leg."

Rose picked up the paper and jabbed a finger at the picture. "Look at this. Jeff Moody took that picture. The article doesn't say why this guy might be the flasher. He just added a random photo to the story. That little weasel is making it up as he goes along."

Daisy shrugged. "He's got to write something and I suppose guesswork is about the best he can do."

"Well, no guesswork for me!" Angela said as she reached into the enormous tote that she was carrying and pulled out her Super-Soaker. "I've got just the thing to catch that pervert. I've put red dye in my squirt gun. I'm going to give him a scarlet letter!"

Chapter Sixteen

Saturday morning was absolutely beautiful. The sky was clear and a light breeze was rustling the leaves. A late night thunderstorm had brought in a cool front and the temperature felt more like late April than late June. Daisy was kneeling beside the patio replacing the zinnias that had been torn out and cursing under her breath. "All my beautiful flowers. If I ever catch this guy he's going to wish he hadn't…"

"Good morning, Daisy. What are you doing there? It's late in the season to be putting flowers in," said Mrs. Hudson.

Daisy jumped. "I didn't see you there!" She stood up and wiped her hands on her shorts. "I'm replacing my zinnia garden. Someone destroyed it the other night."

"Oh my, what happened?"

Daisy moved to the porch and invited Mrs. H. to sit down. "Some idiot tried to flood our house and when they couldn't, they soaked all the furniture and pulled up my flowers. So I'm putting some more in. I don't much like the white, but I guess I was lucky Homestead Gardens still had any zinnias at all."

"You do love those flowers, don't you?"

"Yes. My dad used to plant them when I was little. He wasn't much of a gardener, but he could always get the zinnias to grow. How's everything with you? No one's been bothering you, have they? No stupid pranks?"

"No dear. Not a thing has happened at my house. I'm so sorry for you and Rose. I wonder why you're being picked on. There must be a reason, don't you think? Are you and your sister being nosy again?"

Daisy said. "I don't know what you mean."

Mrs. Hudson smiled. "I don't think your aunt would have approved of you two getting involved in things like murder."

Daisy looked at Mrs. Hudson sitting there on the porch in her housecoat and slippers and smiled. "You remind me of Aunt Lucy sitting there."

Mrs. Hudson laughed, "Do I? I guess old ladies all start to look alike, don't we? I'm so glad that hot spell broke. I thought I'd never be able to get out of the house again."

They heard barking and turned to see Ron Tucker, walking two little dogs across his yard to Daisy's back gate. Daisy grinned and said, "Ron, come on in. What have you got there?"

"Well, you know my Maggie." A small white dog of uncertain parentage wagged her tail and beamed at Daisy and Mrs. H. "She and I wanted to introduce you and Malcolm to our new friend, Rex Harrison."

A beautiful little brown and white English bulldog puppy was standing close to Ron's leg.

Rose started to call Malcolm, but he was already wriggling out of the dog door. He ran over to Maggie to say hello, but stopped short and stood staring at the puppy. He nudged the little guy's head with his own and did a bit of rather intimate doggie sniffing. Then he and Maggie seemed to come to some sort of agreement and they took off running around the yard with Rex Harrison scampering along in back of them.

Daisy laughed, "He's beautiful, Ron.

Ron smiled. "Maggie picked him out. He's got a pedigree as long as your arm. She and I had talked about it. I'm getting up there and so is she. Whoever goes first, we don't want the other to be alone. Isn't he dandy?"

"He certainly is. But you and Maggie shouldn't be talking about going anywhere. You're both full of life!"

Ron turned to Mrs. Hudson and said, "Cute, isn't he?"

"I'll give you that, but you keep him out of my yard. Puppies like to dig and I don't want my tomatoes disturbed!"

"Rose, wait until you see Mr. Tucker's new puppy. He's as cute as he can be."

Rose had just finished a sale and was getting a cold drink. "What kind did he get this time? Mixed mutt with a suggestion of poodle?"

"No! It's a purebred English bulldog!" Ron Tucker had always had a series of, as he called them, hobo hounds. Some were strays that he took in. Others he found at the pound or the vets.

Rose's eyebrows shot up. "Great Dane in the morning! Where did he get the money to do that? A pedigreed bulldog! They cost a small fortune. I've always thought Ron was short of cash. I know the vet gives him a discounted rate. I overheard them talking one day when I took Malcolm in."

"You're right. He hardly ever runs the air conditioning. And now I remember Lucy telling me she knew his house was paid for, but that his only income is social security. So how the heck does he afford another dog, much less a little blueblood like Rex?"

The shop door opened and Tonya came in. She said, "I just saw your ex take Brad Douglas in for questioning. I suppose it's just questioning. He wasn't handcuffed, but he was put in the back seat of the police car."

"Really?" said Daisy. "I wonder if Bill's found out something new."

Rose said, "Tonya, has Tom told you anything?"

"Not a thing. The state guys don't like to share with lowly locals. Oh, but he asked me to tell you he heard from his friend in North Carolina and he'll call you tonight and tell you what he found out."

Rose said, "Great! Hey, why don't you come for dinner? I

need guinea pigs for a new cocktail I'm working on."

"I'd love to. We didn't have anything planned. What can I bring?"

"Not a thing," said Daisy. "I'm running out to the store in a minute. We'll just have something easy on the grill. Rose, why don't you ask Peter and I'll see what Marc's doing.

At seven that evening Rose was in the kitchen mixing a pitcher of cocktails. She turned to Daisy and said, "Peter seemed a bit surprised by the invitation. I think he likes more advance notice. But he's coming."

Daisy was mixing an olive oil, lime juice and garlic marinade for the chicken breasts. She said, "He really is formal, isn't he? Marc's coming, too. He is never formal and never passes up a free meal. Does Peter talk about his family?"

Rose asked, "Some. Why?"

"I just wondered if his whole family is as stuffy as he is."

"Oh. I believe his mother is one of those society women who never put a foot wrong. She sounds pretty intimidating and he's an only child. Didn't talk about Papa, except to call him Papa. He did mention his ex-wife, but only to say she enjoyed escargot."

Daisy poured the marinade over a bowl of chicken breasts and put it in the refrigerator. "Hmm."

Rose handed her a glass and said, "I think this will loosen him up."

Daisy sipped and said, "Mmm. Tasty. What is it?"

"I call it a Good Old Summertime. Vodka and fruit. I went a little heavy on the vodka."

Daisy handed Rose six ears of corn and said, "Well then, before you and I get too looped, we'd better finish fixing dinner. Shuck these and I'll make the slaw."

The evening was lovely. They were able to eat on the patio for the first time in weeks. The corn was sweet, the weather was breezy and the cocktails went down quite easily.

Rose and Peter went in to get the dessert. She came back carrying an apple pie.

Peter had a bottle of champagne and glasses. As he uncorked it he said, "To celebrate."

Daisy asked, "What are we celebrating?"

"Wonderful company. And my escape from the clutches of the law. Your ex-husband seems to have cleared me as a suspect in that woman's murder. I spent a few hours talking to him this morning and he appears to be satisfied with my alibi - I'm shocked that I'm using that term - for the night in question."

"And what was it? Your alibi?" asked Daisy.

"I was at a seminar in Baltimore that Monday and Tuesday. Apparently, Detective Greene finally tracked down some other attendees who vouched for my being there."

"Well, great! But were you really worried? You hardly knew the woman. You didn't even have a motive, did you?"

"Of course, I was worried. It's unpleasant to be suspected of a thing like that. I suppose it was because she and I had that little spat that I came under suspicion. But his attention seems to have shifted to Mr. Douglas."

Marc lifted his glass. He said, "Here's to not being a suspect. I know the feeling well." Marc had been the number one suspect in last year's little murder mystery.

After dinner, Daisy asked Tom to help her with the coffee. As they waited for Mr. Coffee to do its job, she asked him what he'd found out from his friend in North Carolina.

"Well, it's not much of a mystery. Just kind of sad, really. According to the report, Margaret Dove and a group of friends were in Kitty Hawk for a week of vacation. The evening she went missing Margaret told them that she was going out to dinner with a man she'd met that day. She said she'd be back by ten.

"The girls couldn't remember much about him. Margaret left

at seven and never came back. She had her swim suit in her bag. The girls called the police when she hadn't returned by one in the morning. The police assumed that she had just spent the night with this guy, but her friends were adamant that Margaret wouldn't do that.

"And because Margaret was known to swim alone, the cops didn't wait the usual forty-eight hours before starting the search. They didn't find her or any trace of the man she might have been meeting."

Daisy shook her head, "That's terrible. Her poor mother. Not knowing what happened to her."

"Actually, her remains were found a month later. Some fishermen found her all the way down the island in Ocracoke wedged in the sand under a pier. They had to use DNA to identify her. Cause of death was drowning, but she was wearing a sundress. They concluded that she probably was walking in the surf and got caught in a rip current and drowned. Case closed."

"So they never found her date?"

Tom said, "No. Not even sure if she ever met up with him."

"And she wasn't robbed or anything like that?"

Tom leaned against the counter, looked at Daisy and asked, "Robbed? Nothing in the report. Why would you ask that? Daisy, why do you really want to know about Margaret Dove?"

"We're going to North Carolina in August and I remembered the old story and wondered if she'd ever been found."

Tom looked at her for a moment. "Okay. I know you'd tell me if this is something I need to know. Right?"

"Of course."

Late the next morning as Rose was setting the table for lunch with Mattie and Sally, Daisy told her everything Tom had reported.

"That's so sad. But it doesn't sound like a mystery, just a terrible accident."

Daisy shook her head, "I know. But there's the problem of the baseball card. It's really bugging me. How did Brad end up with it?"

"Beats me. Maybe he knows the family. He could be a cousin or something." Rose looked thoughtful as she set a vase with red and white roses on the table. "You know, Margaret Dove's mother might have the answer."

"We could hardly call her out of the clear blue and start grilling her," said Daisy.

"We couldn't, no. But I'll bet Mother could. She's so good with people. They just open up to her. She could just tell Mrs. Dove that we found the baseball card."

"And that we don't have it anymore."

"One bridge at a time."

They heard a commotion in the stairwell. Malcolm, who had been eying the strawberry pie sitting on the sideboard, jumped up and started barking like a little dog possessed. Roscoe hopped off the couch and looked at the door suspiciously. It swung open and Angela came breezing in, holding her squirt gun above her head, followed by Percy. She was laughing hilariously. "I got him!!!! I got him!!!! I got the little pissant!"

"What?" Rose and Daisy cried in unison.

"I was just getting out of the car and I looked up the street and saw that man jogging along. On a Sunday morning, if you please, when really he should be at home meditating on the state of his morals." She patted the squirt gun fondly. "This baby has really got some range. He turned as soon as he saw me, but I got him on the backs of his legs as he ran away."

"Mother, you're crazy! He could have come after you."

"Oh no. Percy was with me. He'd never let anyone hurt me, would you Percy?" Percy looked at her adoringly, then chased the cat out of the room.

Angela continued, "So now the fool *does* have a tattoo on the back of his legs! It dripped down into his shoes. He's a marked man."

"Well, for the moment. But he'll wash it off as soon as he can." asked Rose.

"Oh no, he won't. I bought this dye on-line. It's some sort of commercial stuff that just will not wash off. See, I got a little on my thumb when I was loading the gun and it's still bright red!" She held out her thumb which was, indeed, bright red.

Daisy started laughing. "He's going to rub himself raw trying to get rid of it!"

"Well, it won't work. I tried. Soap, nail polish remover, Comet, Oxy-Clean, nothing gets it off."

Rose said, "Then please put that gun away before you ruin something. Well, now we just have to keep our eyes open for a sleaze ball with red dye on his legs."

Angela's eyes were shining. "We'll find him. I know it!"

"I'm sure we will," said Daisy. "You're a terror with that gun. I think you should let Tom Willis know right away. He really wants to get this guy."

"I will. I'll call him after lunch. He'll be so excited!"

Daisy said, "I'll bet." The doorbell rang. "That must be the ladies. Well, here goes. Remember, we're trying to ferret out information about the old days without letting each of them know that the other is being blackmailed."

Rose added, "And we really are trying to get ready for the Fourth. We've got a lot of work to do."

Chapter Seventeen

Mattie and Sally both looked much happier than the last time the sisters had seen them. Mattie took Rose aside and whispered, "Nothing. I haven't sent any money and he hasn't done a thing. But it doesn't really matter anyway. I talked to Frank and told him everything. He doesn't care a bit about what I did before I met him. He was just upset that I went through it all alone."

She smiled, "Makes me remember why I fell in love with him. But, boy, when he started talking about this blackmailer! I've never seen him so mad."

"I'm so happy to see you back to normal. I think this guy has probably gotten in way over his head. People are getting killed and the police are all over the place. Right now, I think he just wants to get out of Dodge!"

"I hope so. At any rate, he won't be getting any more money from me." Mattie moved to the table and said, "What smells so delicious?"

Lunch was fun. Angela retold her story about shooting the bobber. "That man is quite speedy, but he couldn't outrun my Super Soaker. I really don't understand him at all. If I were he, I'd be afraid of sunburn." She mused a moment, then brightened and said, "Maybe he uses SPF 50. That would take care of things."

Daisy laughed and said, "Who knows. Well, we'd better get to work."

As they were discussing the games for the Fourth, Daisy steered the conversation to the old days. They found out that

Aunt Lucy, Ron Tucker and his wife, Sarah Hudson, and Sally's and Mattie's parents had all been close friends. Sally said, "I remember they were all in and out of each other's houses all the time."

"You're right," said Mattie. "I'd forgotten how close they all were. They played cards every Friday night. It was a ritual. There was another couple, I forget their names, but they moved away years ago. How did we get onto this?"

Daisy said, "I was just wondering what kinds of games they used to have on the Fourth."

Suddenly Angela said, "Cornhole boards!"

Mattie looked puzzled. Daisy asked, "What? That sounds vaguely rude."

"Cornhole boards. It's a game. The ladies and I play it when we go to the *Mighty Wind*. It's kind of like horseshoes, but with bean bags. Lots of fun. It would be perfect!"

Sally said, "Great idea. I should have thought of it myself. My family plays it a lot."

Rose said, "Okay. I guess we could add that. What do we need? Our budget is kind of small."

Angela said, "Not a problem. We just need the boards and bean bags and I'll donate them. I know someone who makes the boards. I'll have him paint them red and green."

"Why red and green, Mother?"

"To look like watermelon. It *is* the Fourth!"

"Hmm. I was just thinking red, white and blue might be the more obvious choice."

Angela looked thoughtful and said, "Oh. Yes. We could do that. And it might be easier than watermelon. Painting all those little seeds could take forever."

Mattie asked, "What's the *Mighty Wind*?"

Angela said, "It's this wonderful sailors' bar in Annapolis where my friends and I go. All the guys know us there! You should come with us one night. We play for Cosmos." Rose stood behind her mother frantically shaking her head.

Mattie laughed and said, "I'll think about it. Well, cornhole boards it is. This should be a good Fourth. I'm looking forward to it."

After Sally and Mattie left, Angela took the dogs for a walk. As they were cleaning up, Rose told Daisy what Mattie had said.

Daisy answered, "That's funny. It's kind of what Sally told me. She talked to her parents and found out they always knew about the jail thing. They went along with her version because that's what she wanted and they were so happy at the changes she'd made in her life. Unfortunately, her fiancée wasn't as kind. They broke up."

Rose looked surprised. "She didn't seem very sad about it. She was in a great mood."

Daisy answered, "She's not. Apparently, they hadn't been getting along for a while and his reaction made her realize why. He's just not a very nice guy. Oh, and she spoke to a lawyer about lying on the loan application. He said it's been over ten years, the loan's been paid back, and nobody is going to care."

Daisy sat at the kitchen table nibbling a piece of the banana bread Mattie had brought. "This is really good. I could probably eat the whole thing. So Sally and Mattie have stopped paying the blackmail and no one has spread any gossip about them."

"I think the blackmailer's lying low and hoping to get out of here without being noticed because *I* think he killed Peggy Merritt. I think she caught him breaking into the post office." said Rose.

"I do, too. Where do we go next?"

"I'm not sure. I thought it was pretty interesting that both Ron and Sarah were friends with the Clovers and the Hendersons. Could one of them be the first blackmailer, do you think?"

"Oh, come on! I can't believe either Ron or Sarah would do something like that. I wish Aunt Lucy were here. She'd know about all of this."

Rose shook her head. "If you're old and broke, you might. And who else would know about the mistakes Sally and Mattie made when they were teenagers?"

Daisy sighed, "I know you could be right. It makes sense. Their parents might have confided in really close friends when their kids were in trouble. But I just hate to think it's one of them."

"Me, too. But I'd like to know where Ron Tucker got the money to buy that dog." Rose suddenly threw the dishtowel across the room. "This stinks."

"Yes it does," agreed Daisy.

Rose thought a minute and said, "Well, let's suppose it is Ron. Then who's the second blackmailer? Because I know for a fact that old Ron Tucker did not attack me that night. Whoever did that was quick and agile. And that's just not Ron!"

"I don't know. I give up. The whole thing makes less and less sense."

Angela walked in with the dogs trailing behind her. "I've been thinking and I think it's time to call Elyse Dove and tell her about the card."

Angela called Elyse Dove that afternoon. They chatted for a long time and when Angela finally put down the receiver there were tears in her eyes. She was quiet for a long time and then said, "I don't know how I would go on if something happened to one of my children."

Rose handed her a glass of wine and said, "Let's go outside and you can tell us about it."

Angela sat between her girls and sipped her wine. She murmured, "Very nice," and put her glass down. "Well, Elyse Dove is a lovely woman who has had more than her share of heartbreak. But she's no fool. I explained who I was and why I was calling. I gave her Tom Willis as a reference. She had me hold the phone while she Googled the Bostwick police department and then called Tom to make sure I wasn't some kind of con artist. Apparently, he put her mind at ease."

Daisy said, "Oh my. I am going to have some explaining to do. I told Tom I was just being nosy. He's going to want to know why you are calling Mrs. Dove."

"Oh don't worry about Tom. I'll take care of him. Anyway, we made plans to have lunch together in Fredericksburg on Wednesday, the four of us."

Daisy said, "What did she say about the card?"

Angela answered, "We didn't talk about it, really. After she was satisfied that I wasn't some sort of crazy lady, we got to talking about our children and the card didn't come up again until we made our lunch date. She said she'd tell us about it then."

Daisy said, "Speaking about the card, I've been thinking. I wonder why Bill took Brad in for questioning? He didn't want to let on that he knew about the blackmail."

"Especially since we don't have the card anymore!" said Rose.

"Exactly. So what do you think he found out? I mean as far as I know, there's no known connection between Brad and Peggy or the post office."

Rose said, "Maybe we could just ask Bill. After all, I am an interested party."

"Bill's not going to tell us anything. He never told me anything about cases when we were married. He'll just use that condescending tone of his and say it's an on-going investigation and 'Daisy, keep your nose out of it.'"

"Okay, then we talk to Brad."

Angela said, "I'm not sure that's a good idea. Brad might very well be the person who attacked you the other night."

Rose said, "All the more reason to talk to him. He won't think we suspect him if we act like we're just concerned about him. I'm going down there tomorrow and see what I can find out."

Daisy said, "I'll go with you. It could be dangerous."

Angela chirped, "Me, too."

Rose shook her head and said, "No, you won't. That would be ridiculous. I'll just drop by in the middle of the day and talk to him. See if he still has the card on display. Ask what Bill wanted. It's a natural enough question. I'll be a couple of shops away in broad daylight. Nothing will happen to me."

"Maybe so," said Angela. "But I don't like it. I'm coming over tomorrow to make sure you stay safe."

Around noon the next day, Rose walked down the street to Yesterday's Heroes. As she got to the door she took out her phone, dialed her mother's line and said, "I'm here. I'm not hanging up. I'll just put the phone in my pocket, so don't start laughing or screaming. He'll hear you."

Angela said, "Of course not, Rose. I wasn't born yesterday. I'm putting you on speaker so Daisy and I can both listen. Now be careful."

Rose pushed open the door to the shop and looked around. She didn't see anyone. She called, "Brad, you here?"

She walked up to the counter. The baseball card wasn't hanging where it usually did. She called again, "Brad, anyone at home?" No answer. She said, "There's no one here, but the door was open. It's kind of spooky. I'm going to take a look in his office."

The phone made a hissing sound and Daisy's voice said, "Just come home. We'll talk to Bill, instead."

"I'm fine. I'm just looking through his desk. Nothing, but old sports junk and bills."

They could hear her opening and closing drawers. Then she said, "Oh, wait. I think this is the frame the card was in. It's…" and then they heard Rose scream and the phone went dead.

Chapter Eighteen

Daisy and Angela raced out their door and down the street. They got to the shop and saw that the door was ajar. Daisy pushed it open slowly. Angela hissed, "Shhh!" as the bell that hung on it jingled. Daisy grabbed it and eased the door shut again. On tiptoe they glided in and silently moved down the aisle to the counter.

Angela whispered, "Rose, sweetie, where are you? Are you all right?"

The office door had swung to, but they could hear sounds coming from behind it. Daisy grabbed a bat from a wall display and said, "Mother, stay here. And be ready to call 911." She moved behind the counter and pushed open the door. Then Daisy burst out laughing.

The office was a bit of a mess. A desk drawer had been pulled out and dumped onto the floor. Rose was just pushing herself off of Bill Greene's stomach, a heavy metal stapler still in her hand. And Bill was laying flat on his back clutching his head.

Rose was saying, "Bill, I am so sorry. I'm just so very sorry. But you really have to stop sneaking up on me like that."

Angela had her squirt gun pointed at Bill. "What did he do to you, Rose? Did he attack you?"

"Mother, put that thing away. You'll stain someone." Rose held out her hand and pulled Bill to his feet. He sat down heavily in the desk chair and dabbed at the cut on his head with a paper towel Daisy had gotten from the bathroom.

Angela said, "No, I won't. Daisy made me wash the dye out.

It's just got plain water in it. Well, what was this man doing attacking you?"

Bill said, "I wasn't attacking anyone. I saw the front door of the shop wide open and heard someone moving around the office. Before I could say, 'Hi Rose. What the hell are you doing breaking into this place?' she turned and hit me with that stapler."

"And then I fell on him when I tripped trying to run out because I didn't realize who it was and I pulled the drawer out as I went down. But I am getting better at self-defense, don't you think?"

Daisy said, "I think he's growling. He used to do that when we were married, mostly after family dinners."

"You didn't like my dinners?" asked Angela.

"The dinners were fine. It was all the rest of it." Bill pulled himself together, sat up straighter in the chair, and said, "Rose, what were you doing in here? And where is Brad Douglas?"

"I have no idea. I came down here to talk to him and the shop was empty. So I thought I'd just leave him a little note. Then you came in and startled me."

"You were going through the drawers. I saw you."

"I was looking for paper."

"Right! And what did you want to talk to him about?"

"I was going to ask him why you had taken him in for questioning. Why did you?"

"You know I can't answer that."

Daisy said, "Oh come on, Bill. The guy might be a murderer and you won't tell us why you questioned him? That's not fair. We could be in danger. And while we're at it, did you really clear Peter?"

Rose smiled charmingly. "You know you're going to tell us eventually. We could have Mother soak it out of you."

Bill shook his head and sighed. "Yes, we cleared Peter Fleming. He was at conference or symposium or some crap like that in Baltimore."

Daisy interrupted, "What about Brad? What did he tell you about the card? Why did you take him in and then let him go?"

Bill put his head in his hands and mumbled something under his breath. Then he looked up and said, "Okay. Okay. If I tell you, will you just shut up?"

"Probably."

"That old man working in the post office now found that a page had been torn out of the binder they keep the post office box information in."

"Oh, the red book. Where Peggy kept track of our payments?"

"Yeah. It's a red book. Well, we finally tracked down which page was missing. It was for the box belonging to Brad Douglas. We also found his fingerprints behind the counter and on the back door. So I picked him up and we had a little chat."

"Oh wow!" said Daisy as she slid the drawer into place and started putting the contents back. "So why did you let him go?"

"There wasn't enough to hold him. He had plausible explanations for the fingerprints. Says the Merritt woman asked him for help with some heavy packages. Alibi-wise, he didn't have much of one. But that's not unusual. We think she was killed about five in the morning. That's when she usually got to work. He says he was home in bed, along with everyone else in this case."

Daisy elbowed Rose and said, "Our plan wouldn't have worked anyway. We got there too late."

Bill frowned. "What wouldn't have worked?"

Daisy was staring into the drawer and said, "Nothing. Not a damned thing. So you let him go?" She held up a roll of brass-colored duct tape from the drawer and said, "Maybe you shouldn't have."

Bill looked at it and said, "Dammit. Daisy you've got your fingerprints all over it. Put it in here." He pulled a plastic evidence bag out of his pocket and Daisy dropped the tape in.

Rose said, "Speaking of post office boxes, did you have any luck finding out about the box next to ours? The one the baseball card should have gone to?"

Bill sighed. "Not yet. The file here was practically illegible and the Office Aide place in Vienna seems to have lost the paperwork. So we're still looking."

Suddenly a voice demanded, "What are you doing in here?" They turned to see Abby Wentworth.

Bill stood up and said, "Better question, Miss - what are you doing here?"

Abby's attitude changed abruptly. She dropped the scowl and simpered, "Oh, I didn't see you there, Billy. Is everything all right?"

Daisy looked at him and said, "Billy? Really?"

"Just why are you here, Ms. Wentworth?"

"I came to meet Brad for lunch. I still want to know why all of you are in his office."

Daisy patted her arm and said, "We all want things, honey." Then she made her way out of the office followed by Rose and Angela. Daisy stopped at the shop door and said, "Billy, come on by when you finish up here. I think we need to talk."

When they got back to the house, Angela said, "I'm hungry. How about you two?" She fixed tuna salad on croissants and fruit. "I don't understand about the duct tape. Why was Bill so interested?"

"Because that was the same kind someone used to tape up Malcolm and rig our front door."

"So it was Brad who broke in here and attacked Rose!"

Daisy thought a minute. "Maybe. It makes a certain amount of sense. It was his baseball card. I've thought all along that he might have been trying to get it back."

Rose said, "But it still comes back to how did he know we

had it?"

"Easy," replied Daisy. "He thinks we're the blackmailers!"

Rose choked on her iced tea as she excitedly waved her hand in the air. "The frame. The card wasn't in it!"

"What?"

"Just before Bill snuck up on me, I found the frame that Brad kept the card in. The stub and scorecard were there, but the card was gone!"

They heard footsteps on the stairs and Bill Greene walked in saying, "It's only me. You left your door unlocked. Are you crazy? There's a killer out there."

Daisy smacked her head, "Hells bells! That was me. Malcolm was in a hurry to get out when we got back here. I forgot to lock the door."

Bill frowned, "Just be more careful, would you?"

"So, did you find Brad?"

"No. And that girl is a menace. I couldn't get rid of her."

"She is a bit clingy if you're a good-looking man," said Daisy. "I guess you qualify."

Bill looked at her thoughtfully for a second. "Well, thanks. I finally got her out of there and took a look around. Nothing-except for the tape. I'll get that printed, but it won't make a difference. It's his tape, in his desk. It'll have his fingerprints on it. So what?"

Daisy said, "It will make a difference if his prints aren't on it!"

Rose asked, "What about the frame?"

"What frame?"

Angela chanted, "The frame with the power. What power? The power of..."

Bill snapped, "Angela!"

"Mother! Due respect to Cary Grant, this is not the time," said Rose. "The frame that the baseball card was kept in. It was under some papers in the bottom drawer. It was empty. So now the real card and the fake card are gone!"

"I didn't see it. I locked the place up when I left. I'll need to get a warrant to get back in if Douglas doesn't turn up." He hit the table with his hand. "Dammit!"

Daisy asked quietly, "Did anyone hear Abby come into the shop? I know I closed the door. The bell should have jingled. I didn't hear it."

They looked at each other and Rose said, "I didn't hear anything, but there was a lot of commotion."

Bill said, "Are you suggesting that she was already in the building? Where? And why would she hide?"

"I don't know. I'm just saying she's a weird girl and I didn't hear the bell when she came in."

Tuesday they opened the shop at ten. Daisy walked over to the post office to check their box and came back over an hour later.

"I dropped by Brad's to see if he's back. Bill was in there, but no sign of Brad."

"Did he find anything?"

"No. Nothing. In fact, the frame was gone and he's furious. He actually had the nerve to suggest that you and I had something to do with it. I told him not to be an ass."

"Brad probably came back and took it. How did Bill get in?"

"He got a warrant and had a locksmith let him in."

The phone rang and Rose answered. She listened for a while and beamed. "I'd love to. Saturday's fine. It's black tie? Oh, what fun! I'm looking forward to it. See you at eight."

Rose put the phone down and said, "I need to go to Nordstrom's."

"Black tie? Where's he taking you? This is kind of late notice, don't you think?"

"Who cares? It's a big affair at the University. I need something long and elegant. And time to shop, so do you mind if

I take the afternoon off? Or better yet, come with me. I'll need a second opinion."

"Sure, I'll go." Daisy sighed, "It's probably as close to going somewhere elegant as I'm going to get any time soon. Marc's idea of a dressing up is wearing a sports coat with his jeans. We'll go after lunch when Tonya gets in."

"Great. I'll probably need shoes, too."

"So you're comfortable going out with Peter?"

"Yes. Why wouldn't I be?" She looked at Daisy and said, "What, you still don't believe Peter had anything to do with Peggy's murder, do you?"

Daisy hesitated and then shrugged her shoulders a little. "No. Not really. If Bill cleared him, I guess I'm good with that. It's just that I don't entirely trust him. Bill's right about that. He does seem to be around at the strangest times."

"Well, I do trust him. And I'm going to a ball. Don't you dare go raining on my parade!"

Chapter Nineteen

Wednesday, Daisy, Rose, and Angela drove to Fredericksburg. Rose parked the car in the public lot and they walked up the street to a restaurant called Sammy T's. A small, pleasant looking woman with curly grey hair was standing outside obviously waiting for someone. Angela walked up to her and said, "Elyse?"

The woman turned and looked at her. "Angela? You made it." She gave Angela a quick hug. "I feel like I know you already."

"I do, too. Elyse, these are my daughters, Rose and Daisy."

They went into the restaurant. It was cool and softly lit. The waitress showed them to a booth and took their drink orders.

"Well, here we are." Elyse took a folder out of her bag and put it on the table. She put her hand over it protectively and said, "Maybe we should order first and then talk. The food here is rather good." They looked over the menu, and were ready to order when the waitress came back with the drinks.

They sat a moment stirring their iced teas. Finally Daisy looked at the folder and said, "Thank you so much for meeting with us. I'm afraid this must be hard for you. I know Mother told you about the baseball card. We're trying to figure out how it got to Old Towne."

She and Rose told Elyse the whole story starting with the blackmail. They told her about the murder, about Brad having the card in his shop, and then finding it in their mail and, finally, having it stolen when someone broke in.

Elyse said, "Thank God you're all right. You could have been killed. And all for a baseball card?"

"Well, it's a very valuable baseball card, as I'm sure you know."

"I don't really. I know it's worth something, but it was always just Bob's card. He was so proud of it. That was one of the happiest days of his life. He loved to tell people about meeting Mickey Mantle.

"Our son Carl never cared for baseball. But Bob and Margaret loved baseball so much. She was a regular encyclopedia of baseball trivia. The two of them could talk about it for hours. She even played Little League until the boys outgrew her. So when Bob died I gave the card to her."

She stopped and sighed. "It's still hard to talk about. She and some girlfriends used to vacation together. That fall a big baseball card show was being held right there in Nags Head the same week she and her friends would be there. Margie took the card with her so she could show it off. She loved telling that story as much as her dad did."

Their lunches arrived and they ate in silence for a few minutes, giving Elyse time to recover. She finally continued the story.

"I take comfort in the fact that she was having a wonderful week. She called me every day. She was so happy. She'd run into a professor of hers who was staying at the hotel and she said it was a real eye-opener because he always seemed so stiff in class. But he invited her to lunch and they had a great conversation about philosophy. That was her major. He offered to be her mentor. She was thrilled."

Daisy started to say something, but stopped herself. She didn't want to interrupt Elyse's train of thought.

Elyse took a deep breath, shook her head, and said, "And then she met someone. She didn't say much. She never did tell me too much about the boys she dated. Not until she was ready to bring them home to meet me. She was so private that way. But I could tell she thought he was someone special."

"Where did she meet him?" asked Rose.

"I'm pretty sure it was at the card show."

She pushed the folder to the middle of the table. "I brought everything the police had on the case. Bob had a good friend on the force, so I was able to get copies of everything. I made this set for you.

Angela glanced at the folder and said, "So what did the police think happened?"

"They couldn't find any trace of her that evening after she left the girls. Her best friend, Susan Murphy, couldn't remember the young man's name. None of them had met him. The police checked all the restaurants and bars on the island. No one had seen her that evening.

"Carl went down there and searched for her. But he had no more luck than the police. Finally, he and they concluded that she must have decided to go swimming either before her date, or with her date, and gotten in trouble and drowned. Some fisherman found her weeks later far down the island. They identified her through DNA. I still can't believe it."

The waitress came by and asked if there was anything else and Daisy said, "Yes. We'll all have vodka tonic, I think." She looked at Elyse sitting there gazing at nothing. "And go light on the tonic."

As they sipped their drinks, Rose picked up the folder and opened it. She paged through a copy of the police report, statements from the girls, weather conditions that evening, and some pictures of Margaret and her friends. She flipped through to the back and gasped. She was looking at 'crime scene photos' of Margaret's body lodged under the steps of a pier that crossed over a sand dune leading to the beach.

Elyse said, "I know. I'm sorry I should have warned you about the pictures. I insisted that the police give me everything they had because I knew in my heart it was something more than an accident. And with what you tell me about this man having the baseball card, well, I guess I was right."

Rose said, "Elyse, this will all go to Bill Greene, the detective in charge of the case at home. He's a good detective. He'll get to the bottom of this. I know he will."

Angela added, "And in the meantime, we'll stay in touch. I want you to know what's happening."

As they said good-bye outside the restaurant, Daisy said, "Elyse, where did Margie go to school?"

"George Washington University. She was so proud of that." She turned away again and they watched as she walked slowly down the street toward her home.

Rose said, "Let's take a walk. I need cheering up and that drink is making me sleepy. I want to be alert for the drive home."

They walked along Caroline Street and checked out several antique stores. They stopped at the Virginia Store and got some of the hot pepper jelly Angela liked. Then they treated themselves to ice cream cones sitting in the shade of a tree outside the shop.

Rose said, "Okay. Enough eating! We're going to hit rush hour traffic if we don't get a move on."

No one spoke as they left Fredericksburg and headed back toward Route 301. They were crossing the Potomac again when Daisy finally said, "Well, there's a mighty big elephant in the room."

Rose stared out the window at the towering smokestacks marring the Maryland shoreline and sighed. "I don't want to talk about it."

"Well, we need to. Peter could be the professor Margaret met on vacation."

"Or it could be someone else. There must be a ton of

philosophy teachers at GW. Besides, even if Peter knew her, it's much more likely that the man she met at the card show was her date for that night."

"That's true. I just think it's strange that Peter seems to show up everywhere."

"I think it's strange that you latch onto Peter when it's obvious that Brad Douglas must be the man she met at the card show!"

"You're right. I think he must be. But you're not going out with Brad."

Angela said, "Quiet. Both of you. We have no evidence that Peter met Margaret Dove. He may have or not. Even if he did, the meeting didn't sound at all sinister. And Bill feels that Peter is no longer under suspicion. But Brad having the card is very suspicious. I wonder where he is right now."

They were almost home driving down Market Street when Angela said, "Pull over Rose and let's see if Brad's back in his shop."

Rose parked the car and they all got out. The shop was locked up tight, only the glow from the exit sign could be seen inside. Angela said, "Let's look around in back."

They walked down the alley to the back of the building. The door was locked. Rose looked in the window next to it, but couldn't see anything. As she turned away her foot slipped and she lost her balance. She put her hand on the window to catch herself and nearly fell over when the glass fell away and crashed to the floor inside. "Whoa Nelly! How did that happen?"

Daisy was examining the window. "It looks like someone cut the glass out and stuck it back in. See, there's chewing gum stuck on the edge here holding the glass in place."

Angela said, "This must be how they got in to steal the frame."

Daisy said, "I guess. But you know what? Right now, I just don't care. It's been a long, sad day and I'm really tired. Let's go home and have a little dinner and a drink. I feel the need of liquid comfort."

While they were waiting for pizza to be delivered, Rose made a pitcher of Sangria. By the time the pizza arrived they were already a bit mellow. After the second pitcher they felt good enough to call Bill and tell him about their day.

Daisy made the call to his cell. When he answered, they put him on speakerphone so they could all tell him the story.

Bill finally shouted, "What the hell have you all been drinking? Would you please take me off speaker? I can't hear you."

Daisy said, "Oh, all right," and picked up the handset. She told him about their meeting with Elyse Dove and about the loose window at the sports shop. Then she said, "We sort of promised Elyse that you'd find out who killed her daughter."

"Well that was a dumb thing to promise. Not my case, not even my state!"

"I know." She hung up the phone, yawned, and said, "I think aspirin and bed sounds about right. Mother, stop that. I'll take care of the dishes. You look tired. Do you still want to walk with us in the morning? We usually leave at seven."

"You bet. I'll be good to go by morning." She finished putting the plates in the dishwasher and turned to the stairs. "Rats, I forgot to bring my book. I guess I'll have to wait to see who done it. Nighty-night, sweethearts."

Rose said, "I'll just let the mutts out for a minute, then I'll be up."

As Rose stood on the back porch waiting for the three furry friends to pee, she could smell cigarette smoke on the night breeze. Suddenly, she felt uneasy standing there by herself, in the dark. Roscoe must have, too. He hissed and ran inside. Then Malcolm and Percy barked sharply and ran in after him. Rose closed and locked the door and checked the alarm system. Then she and the boys made the rounds checking all the other windows and doors. Reassured that everything was locked up tight, but still uneasy, she made her way up to bed.

Chapter Twenty

Daisy yawned, rolled her shoulders, then groaned. "This is good. Really. Up early, brisk walk, just what I need. What did you put in that sangria, anyway?"

"A little wine, a little vodka. Maybe a little more vodka than absolutely necessary," replied Rose as she rubbed her temples. "I think it's the fruit. Booze and fruit really don't mix."

"Okay, I'll go with that. It was the fruit."

They were walking slowly along the path. Malcolm and Percy were close behind, dragging their tails and sitting down for a breather every few minutes.

"Come on you two. If I can keep going, so can you," said Daisy. "We probably shouldn't have given the dogs quite so much fruit."

"You're right. We shouldn't have. We should take them home right now and let them sleep it off."

Angela, who was bouncing along the path well ahead, called back to them, "Move it, girls. It's a beautiful day. Get with the program!"

"Oh my God, how does she do it?"

They finally reached their turn around point. Angela, wearing tennis whites and a bright turquoise headband, was jogging in place waiting for them. "Well, you two clearly inherited your father's metabolism. Let's go. Walk it off."

As they turned into the lane leading to their house, they met Abby Wentworth jogging toward them. "You girls are out early."

"Just barely. I wish I felt as energetic as you look. Have a good run," said Daisy as she watched Abby run by. She turned to Rose and said, "How the hell does she do it? She even carries those walking weights. Lord, I can barely carry my arms!"

"She's young."

"Not all that young. She must be twenty-eight or so."

"Well, she's younger than I am! I have to believe youth gives her an edge or I'll have to admit that I'm a complete mess physically."

When they got to the house, they met Roscoe sauntering up their driveway with something trailing out of his mouth. He walked up to Daisy and dropped it at her feet - a sprig of ivy. "A present? For me? Well, thank you, Roscoe." She picked it up and said, "Where did you get this? Ooh, and what did you drag it through?"

Rose said, "Must have been from the fence behind the garage. That's the only ivy we've got. What's with those two?"

She looked at Malcolm and Percy who were at the gate to the backyard. They were hopping up and down and growling. Angela walked down the driveway and opened the gate. The dogs raced along the fence that separated their yard from Ron Tucker's. They stopped short at the rear of the garage and really lost it, howling like their lives depended on it.

Rose stomped into the yard and said, "What is your problem? No more fruit for you. And my head aches, so quiet."

Daisy stood next to Rose looking at the ivy Roscoe had dropped. She said, "Rose, I don't think it's the fruit that's upsetting them. I think it's the ivy. That looks like blood on it."

Mrs. Hudson came out on her porch and called loudly, "What on earth is going on over there? Is everything all right? Your dogs are waking up the neighborhood."

At that moment Angela, who had gone over to the dogs to settle them down, let out a terrified scream. Her legs seemed to give out and she thumped down onto the grass pointing to the back of the garage.

"Mother, are you all right?" They ran over to her. Angela was shaking and said, "Look."

Daisy and Rose turned to see a body wedged into the small space between the garage and the fence. Rose felt for a pulse and drew her hand back quickly. She said, "Well, we found Brad Douglas and he is most definitely dead."

Chapter Twenty-One

"This is too much! I can't believe it. Another body. You can't swing a dead cat around here without tripping over one!" Daisy was sitting in the kitchen with her mother and Rose while crime scene techs swarmed over the yard.

Rose said, "Exactly." She looked over at her mother who had been holding Percy tightly and staring blankly out the window. "Drink your tea, Mother. I put lots of sugar in it."

Angela sat down and picked up her cup. "I'm fine, girls. It was just such a shock to see him there. But I'm good now. I just don't want to think about it." She picked up the Bostwick Bulletin started paging through it.

"Look at this." She was staring at an article in the paper. "It seems the bobber has moved on to College Park."

Daisy said, "You must have scared him off. Go Angela!"

"But I wanted to catch him, not scare him off someplace else. Really! This just burns my toast."

Daisy said, "Toast. I could eat toast. I'm hungry. What is Bill doing, anyway?"

They had been waiting for Bill for well over an hour. Tom Willis had shown up first and secured the scene. He had called the state police and their people started streaming in. Rose put a closed sign on the shop door and called Tonya and told her not to come in.

Bill Greene finally got there at eleven. He was not in a good mood. "Okay, which one of you killed that guy?"

Daisy said, "Is that supposed to be funny? It's not."

"No, it's not supposed to be funny. I'm serious. Did one of you club that guy to death?"

Angela looked like she might be sick and Rose said, "Bill, this is hard enough. Don't be an ass and make it worse. No, I didn't kill Brad and neither did Daisy or my mother. Happy?"

"What happened? Tell me from the beginning."

They told him about the dogs finding the body. Rose said, "That's it. We found the body and called the police. What did you expect us to do?"

"You are all so loony, I never really know what you'll do."

"Charming as usual," said Daisy "You just can't help being a jerk, can you, Bill?"

Rose asked, "He was clubbed to death, like Peggy Merritt?"

"Looks that way."

"When was he killed?"

"First guess, sometime around midnight."

"Did they find any cigarettes near the body?"

"Why?"

"Because when I let the dogs out at eleven I thought I could smell cigarette smoke. It kind of spooked me and the dumb chums."

"Yes, there was a cigarette butt near the body."

Rose held her head in her hands. "I was standing in the yard with a killer!"

Daisy pushed herself out of her chair and said, "I need to get out of here. Is it any reason we can't go out to lunch?"

"Not that I can think of. Go to lunch. You can talk to all your fans."

Rose asked, "What are you talking about?"

"There are a ton of lookie-loos out front, including that pain-in-the-ass reporter."

Daisy said, "Oh great. Jeff Moody hounding us again - just what we need. Is there any way you can arrest him for being obnoxious?"

"I would if I could. I'll be back to talk some more after I find out what the techies discover."

Rose looked out the window. "We could go out the sunroom door and hop Mrs. Hudson's fence and leave through her yard."

Daisy said, "And what do we do then? Put on false mustaches and sneak back to our car?"

Angela perked up, "We could you know. Maybe not mustaches, but we could go out in disguise. It would be fun."

Daisy said, "I am not dressing up to hide from some idiot reporter. Let's just face the music."

Rose said, "All right. We'll be brave and go out the front door."

They took the dogs with them having decided to pick up sandwiches at the deli and let the dogs run in the park while they ate. They no sooner got out the door than Jeff Moody ran up to them. "Okay, what's the story? The old lady next door says you found a body. What about it? Who'd you find? Does this have anything to do with the post office murder? The cops won't tell me anything."

Rose shook her head and said, "No comment. Talk to the police and leave us alone."

"Oh, come on. You gotta give me something." He blocked her way to the sidewalk. "My job depends on this and whether or not I can get a decent scoop."

Rose said, "Jeff, please, it's been a horrible morning. Just let us get by, would you?"

"I will as soon as you give me a story." Rose tried to move past him, but he got right up in her face. Malcolm started growling and Moody made the mistake of kicking him.

Angela swung into action with her squirt gun at the same time Percy attacked his leg. By the time he got away from them, Moody was soaking wet and his pants leg was in tatters.

He backed out of the yard and yelled, "You're all freaking nuts!" As he trotted down the street, the three women stared in amazement at the streaks of red dye running down the back of his calf.

Rose muttered, "Good golly Miss Molly! It's the bobber."

Daisy said, "Wow! Who'd have guessed our local reporter?" They were sitting in the park eating corned beef sandwiches and watching the dogs chase each other. "What do we do now?"

Angela said, "I've already called Tom Willis and asked him to meet us here. He's on his way."

Rose said, "This day just gets better and better! A dead body and the bobber. Did either of you see Peter? I wanted to talk to him."

Daisy said, "Me, too. Rose, he could well be the professor that Margaret Dove met in North Carolina."

"We don't know that. There must be a hundred philosophy professors she could have met. Besides, Brad had the card. He must be the one who stole it."

"Not a hundred. I checked. There are only about ten philosophy professors at G.W. right now. It's not a really big department. And, you're right. Brad had the card, but now he's dead. Somebody killed him - and then stole the card. Who else was in North Carolina?"

"Well, you're quite the buttinski, aren't you? I'm not a child, Daisy. I think Peter is a really nice guy. And I have good instincts about people. Better than yours sometimes."

"What does that mean?"

"Well, you married that cheating, rat-bastard Bill Greene."

Daisy opened her mouth to say something, but then laughed. "Fair enough. I definitely picked a winner there, didn't I? But good instincts or not, I still want you to be careful. You shouldn't be alone with him until these murders are solved, just in case you're wrong and he's a closet whack-a-doodle."

"Well, I won't be."

"How is that? You're going out Saturday night."

"Yes, we are. But he's sending a car with a driver for me. And there will be a million people at the affair and then the driver will bring me home. I'll be fine. And I'm right about him anyway."

Angela lit up at the mention of a car and driver. "A limousine and driver? Divine. What an elegant night you'll be having. I can just see you gliding around the ballroom in Peter's arms to the strains of the Blue Danube waltz. Oh, what bliss! And then a moonlight stroll through the garden. The subtle scent of jasmine in the air and a nightingale singing sweetly. And then a sudden cloudburst and you'll have to run into the gazebo and you'll laugh until he takes you in his arms and smothers you with burning kisses!" She looked wistfully into the sky and sighed.

Rose stared at her mother and said, "What have you been drinking? This is Peter were talking about."

But Daisy put her arm around Angela and said, "Not to worry, Mother. We'll be having fun, too. I've got a surprise planned."

"Does it involve dancing in the moonlight?"

"Almost." At that moment, Tom Willis pulled up and got out of his car. "What's up? You said it was urgent."

Angela told him about spotting the dye on Jeff Moody's legs and about the article in the morning's paper. "We've got him, Tom. Now you can just go arrest him."

"It's not that easy, Angela. I can't arrest him for having red dye on his legs. But now I know who to watch. And I've already heard from the police in College Park. I'll be talking to them again this afternoon.

"Meanwhile, please do not say anything to him or try to catch him."

Rose and Daisy said, "Of course not. It's all up to you now."

Angela was quiet. Tom said, "Angela, I mean it. We know he's the flasher. He could also be the murderer. Just let me take care of it. Okay?"

"Oh, okay."

"Promise me you'll leave him alone."

"I promise that I won't try to catch him. But if he kicks one of our pets again, all bets are off."

Chapter Twenty-Two

Absolutely elegant in a deep-cranberry gown, shirred at the waist and gently ruffled at the neckline, Rose walked into the living room, twirled around and said, "Tada!"

"Wow!" Ron Tucker exclaimed as he sat with Angela on the couch. "Who's the lucky fellow?"

Angela said, "Rose is going out with Peter Fleming tonight. He's sending a car for her. Isn't that romantic?"

"Well, I don't know. Seems kind of impersonal to me. Any young man lucky enough to have Rose accept his invitation should be escorting her from this very door himself."

Rose smiled, "Ron, you're very sweet. Peter may be lucky, but he's also on the planning committee and needs to be at the hotel long before the party starts. He will be escorting me home in person."

"I should hope so. You do look like a dream, I must say. That dress is something. You'll put the other ladies to shame."

"Are the earrings all right? Not too much?" Rose asked as she watched the diamond clusters twinkle in the mirror over the fireplace.

Daisy walked into the room and said, "Not at all. They're perfect. And this will match." She handed Rose a bracelet. "The only thing that idiot I married ever gave me that was worth keeping."

Rose slipped the diamond bracelet onto her arm. "It's beautiful." The doorbell rang and Daisy ran down to answer it.

Sally Henderson came up the stairs behind her carrying a

small box that she handed to Rose. "Peter ordered this for you and asked me to deliver it myself. He was very specific. I think it's rather nice. I hope you like it."

Rose opened the box and said, "Oh, it's lovely." She held a nosegay of dusty pink and white roses and tiny tendrils of ivy. "Peter chose the flowers?"

"He did, indeed. There's a boutonniere for him, too. Boy, you look gorgeous."

Rose giggled. "I feel gorgeous."

The doorbell rang again and she said, "That should be my ride." Sure enough Daisy came back up the stairs followed this time by a uniformed chauffer who introduced himself, then took Rose's arm and escorted her to the black town car sitting at the curb. Of course everyone followed her out of the house.

Rose shook her head and said, "You'd think I've never had a date before. Go back inside. This looks crazy. And don't wait up for me." She was just getting into the car when Mrs. Hudson and Abby came out onto the porch to watch. Then Mary Newhart ran across the street shouting, "Wait. I want a picture."

Angela said, "Oh me, too! How could I forget?" Rose got out of the car and posed next to the chauffer while Angela pulled out her cell phone and she and Mary took pictures. Rose was feeling a little ridiculous. "This is absurd. I'm not sixteen and this isn't a prom. Enough already, I'm going to be late."

But Abby grabbed her hand to look at the bracelet. Angela kept snapping pics. Malcolm and Percy were sniffing the driver's leg who stood there looking like he was wondering if kicking dogs would get him fired.

Daisy was enjoying the whole pageant, but finally said, "Okay everybody, knock it off. Rose will be late and this poor guy," she looked at the chauffer, "will probably get in trouble if she is."

Rose got into the car and the chauffer, with a visible sense of relief, hopped into the driver's seat and took off.

As Daisy and Angela sat in the sunroom eating mushroom and green olive pizza and watching the dogs playing in the yard, Daisy filled her mother's glass with a frothy orange concoction.

Angela took a sip. "Mmm, very tasty. What did you call this?"

Daisy smiled and said, "I call it a Midnight Marauder. It suits this evening's plan."

Angela's eyes lit up. "What have you got in mind?"

"Well, as I said, I do trust Rose's instincts about Peter – at least about his not attacking her. And I trust Bill."

Angela snorted, "You most certainly do not!"

"His police instinct – I trust his police instinct. He's positive that Peter couldn't have had time to get back from Baltimore, kill Peggy and return in time for a seven o'clock seminar. Who in God's name schedules a seminar for seven in the morning after a cocktail party the night before? These academics must be real masochists. But something about that man is strange. Why would he spend so many nights in that bookstore when he has that beautiful house downtown?"

"To be near Rose?"

"He hardly ever sees Rose when he's there. No, he's up to something and I want to know what. So, I thought we'd take this excellent opportunity, while he and Rose are both occupied for the entire evening, to check out his attic!"

Angela clapped her hands like a little kid. "Super! I happen to have suitable late night attire right upstairs."

"I thought you might. We'll go around eleven after Ron takes his dogs out. In the meantime, I want to have a good look through all the papers that Elyse Dove gave us."

"I thought you gave them to Bill to investigate."

"With all the commotion finding Brad's body, I forgot. Which is okay because we never really got to look through everything properly."

They spent the next hour reading the police reports on Margaret Dove's disappearance and looking at the wretched crime scene photos and the much happier pictures of Margaret with her friends at the beach.

"I don't see anything that would help us here. I'm just going to give it all to Bill and hope he can figure it out," said Daisy.

Angela said, "I just can't get over this. I don't know how Elyse Dove does it."

She was studying one picture. She held it out to Daisy. "Look at this. The girls look so happy, but something seems off."

Daisy took the picture and examined it. "What? I don't see anything. It's Margaret and her girlfriends standing on an old pier."

"I can't put my finger on it, but there's something about this picture."

Daisy looked again and said, "I still don't see anything. You know what? I'm going to scan all of this into the computer before I give it to Bill."

"Good idea. After you scan it in, email it to me, would you? I want to figure out what's bothering me."

"Will do. I know it'll come to you."

At eleven, Daisy was standing on a stepstool at the back of her closet pulling out an old tote bag. She checked the contents. WD-40, screwdrivers, kitchen tongs, a large black scarf, and two flashlights were right where she left them after her last midnight caper. She tested the flashlights, replaced the batteries in one of them, and said to Angela, "It's all good. Let's go."

They stood at the window and watched Ron Tucker walk his dogs past their house and waited ten minutes until he walked back on his way home. Then Daisy, 'burglar bag' over her shoulder, and Angela slipped quietly out of the side door and up the driveway.

Just as they got to the street the door of Clover Tavern opened and a group of people came out laughing and talking loudly as they walked to their cars.

"Rats! Maybe we should wait until the Tavern closes," whispered Daisy as she backed down the driveway. "People can see Peter's gate from the Tavern door."

"Not to worry. We'll just go around back and hop Mrs. Hudson's fence. Then we can slip across the street and go down the alley next to Marc's place. We can sneak into Peter's yard from the other side. There aren't any lights back there and nobody can see the back of the book store anyway."

Daisy was impressed. "You didn't just think of this, did you, Mother?"

"I like to have contingency plans. When you told me about this evening's scheme I sort of scouted out all the routes in my head. So let's go for it. I mean, what's the worst that could happen? If someone stops us, we'll just say we're out for a walk."

Daisy looked at her mother standing in the dark wearing black tennis shoes, black leggings, black gloves, and a black jacket with the hood pulled low over her face. "Somehow, I just don't think the police would buy that. You look like a second story man."

"Pish. I just like to dress for the occasion."

"Exactly my point!"

"Nobody is going to see us. That's my point. Come on, Daisy. It's getting late and Rose will be home before we know it."

"Oh. Okay. Let's go."

They backed down the driveway and crossed the yard. Daisy was saying, "Let me help you over the fence," just as Angela vaulted over it in an effortless leap.

Daisy's jaw dropped open.

"Yoga! Keeps me fit. Close your mouth before you swallow a fly," purred Angela.

"Yoga, huh! Who knew?" Daisy scrambled over with

considerably less grace. They crossed the yard silently and crept up the driveway to the street, waiting a moment at the curb to make sure all was quiet. Mrs. Hudson's lights stayed off and no one was outside the Tavern.

Daisy and Angela crossed the street avoiding the light from the streetlamp. They ran down Elm and turned into the alley running behind Lost Treasures. Finally they came to the small gate that opened into the back garden of the Book Renew. As Daisy pulled the gate, it squeaked loudly. She got out the WD-40 and sprayed, waited a moment, then tried the gate again. It opened silently and they tiptoed through the mounds of daisies and sweet smelling herbs growing across the back of the property.

As they neared the shop, Daisy ran into what must have been one of the last remaining metal trash cans in the state of Maryland. She murmured, "Perfect," and dragged it over to the side of the shed. While she used it to climb up to the roof, Angela got a toehold on the brick and, once again, effortlessly pulled herself up.

Daisy shook her head in wonder and muttered, "Really?"

They were on the roof of the shed when the full moon came out from behind a cloud. Daisy whispered, "Wow. That moon's bright! Now we carefully creep over to the porch roof and get into the attic window from there. But this time you're not our look-out, so we go slowly and keep low."

The last time she had sneaked into this particular attic, Rose had been with Daisy and Angela had stayed at the house to keep an eye out which had proved to be a lifesaver.

Angela said, "We should be all right. Ron's finished walking the dogs and nobody could see us in these clothes." She glanced at Daisy's blue jeans and long sleeved navy tee. She pulled a dark scarf out of her pocket and said, "Here, put this on and cover up your hair. It shines-which in any other case is something to treasure. But not here. Now we need to be very quiet."

They shimmied up to the window, but a dark shade prevented them from seeing in. Daisy said, "I hope the window isn't locked."

"What do we do if it is?"

"Go home. Mother, I'm not about to break in. I do have my own moral code. I figure if an entrance is unlocked, it's fair game. But I won't actually break a window."

"I will."

"No, you won't. Anyway, we won't need to." She slid the window open quietly. They pushed past the shade and slipped in. Daisy turned on her flashlight giving just enough illumination to guide Angela to the light switch. Suddenly the attic was filled with hundreds of little twinkling lights running back and forth across the ceiling.

They looked around the room and Angela gasped. Daisy said, "Wow!"

Angela replied, "Exactly."

Chapter Twenty-Three

Angela said, "Oh my goodness," as she walked from poster to poster. They were standing in a room completely devoted to B movies, especially spaghetti westerns. *The Good, the Bad, and the Ugly* autographed by Lee Van Cleef. The rest of the Dollar Trilogy posters signed by Clint Eastwood and the director, Sergio Leone. One wall held movie memorabilia from the Zapata Westerns, including an original script from Damiano Damiani's *A Bullet for the General*.

And the crowning glory of the room was a seventy-two inch HD TV mounted on the third wall. A leather recliner was placed directly in front of it on the other side of the room. And a bookcase lined the rear wall holding hundreds of DVDs of lousy B movies, including *Rocky*.

Beside the chair was a small refrigerator. Daisy opened the refrigerator to find bottles of Yoo-Hoo and Gatorade. She started giggling.

Angela hooted when she opened a cupboard full of every Tastycake snack cake known to man. Not to mention Twinkies, Sno-balls, Little Debbie's, marshmallow peeps, and those horrible orange candy peanuts. There was also a decent selection of Twizzlers, Sno-Caps, root beer barrels, sour balls, and various other movie theatre treats.

Angela said, "No popcorn machine. I'm disappointed."

Daisy gasped, "He's a secret junk-food, junk-movie junkie!!! I love it." They were practically rolling on the floor laughing when Daisy said, "Why here? He has a perfectly good house of his own. Why hide this stuff here?"

"Yes, why here? That's exactly what inquiring minds want to know."

"You know what would really put the icing on the Tastycake? If he lives with someone who won't let him indulge his passion at home."

Angela stiffened. "You think he's married and dating Rose at the same time. I'll sick Percy on him!"

Daisy smiled sweetly and said, "No, I don't think he has a wife. I'm thinking he has a mother!"

Angela and Daisy did wait up for Rose. They cuddled up on the couch with a nice little Pinot Gris and watched *Field of Dreams*. They were well into *The Natural* when they heard a car pull up outside. A minute later Rose came up the stairs alone.

"No Peter?" asked Angela.

"He went home. It's late. Why are you still up?"

"We wanted to see how the night went," asked Daisy. "Did you have a good time?"

Rose sat down, slipped off her sandals, and put her feet up on the table. "I did - for the most part. I met Colin Powell and his wife! And the president of the university and a couple of senators. Peter does move in a sort of rarefied atmosphere. And the music was wonderful and Peter is a great dancer. So that was good. And we had dessert at the Old Ebbitt Grill which was nice-ish. And then we stopped by his house on the way back here."

Daisy said, "Woo-woo!"

"Not so much. We stopped by so we could take his mother home."

Daisy looked surprised and said, "Really? His mother was at the party?" She gave Angela a nudge. "And she lives with him?"

"Just until her new home is finished. Apparently, she sold her house in Georgetown and is having one built on the Bay somewhere. She's been at Peter's for six months already. And it looks like she'll be there at least another six."

Angela asked, "What's she like? You don't sound too enthusiastic."

"Well, she is really beautiful, if you like tall, slim and steely. She sort of dominates the room, if you know what I mean - but not in a good way. What is this?" Rose picked up the pitcher of Midnight Marauders and poured herself a glass.

Daisy said, "It's a little concoction I mixed up for this evening."

Rose took a sip and said, "It's good." Rose leaned back and twirled the orange liquid in her glass meditatively. "I can't see this woman whooping it up with her girlfriends. Or even quietly enjoying whatever this is." She took another sip. "She seemed to find most things distasteful. She sent her Peach Crumble back at the restaurant which truly annoyed the waiter. I can see now where Peter gets some of his ideas."

Daisy said, "Me, too. Did he order dessert?" Angela started tittering and Daisy giggled, "Stop that, Mother."

Rose looked puzzled and said, "No. It was late and he really doesn't eat a lot of sweets." Daisy and her mother burst out laughing.

Rose demanded, "Okay, what the hell is going on?"

"I guess it's time to fess up." Angela pulled out her cell phone, brought up the photo album and said, "Just look at this!" Rose scrolled through shots of Peter's attic -TV, candy cupboard, refrigerator contents, and movie shelf.

"Where did you get these pictures?"

"In the attic of Peter's bookshop," said Daisy. "We had a little adventure ourselves this evening. I know. I know. I know. It was totally wrong. But I really thought Peter might be up to something rotten. And Mother and I decided we had better find out just what he gets up to in the shop." She got very serious and pronounced, "And, I'm sorry to say this, it's not good."

Rose stood up, hands on her hips, and stared at them. "I

cannot believe you would do this!"

She paced around the room a moment, then said, "What am I saying? Of course I can believe you would do this. You really had no business spying on him. You do know that, don't you?"

Her mother shook her head and said, "Rose, calm down. We were only thinking of your safety. He could have been some sort of drug fiend or bomb maker. Daisy even thought he could be entertaining prostitutes. But, we're all relived to know, it's nothing of the sort."

Daisy hooted, "No, he's just a pompous hypocrite who loves bad movies and junk food! He probably didn't order dessert because they don't serve Moon Pies at Old Ebbitt's!"

Rose started to get all huffy, but then started laughing. "That little rat! He's been trying to make me eat raw fish and snails."

"That's not all," said Angela. "He has all six of the Rocky films! I lined them up and took a picture for you."

Rose looked at the picture Angela was showing her. "Boy, this really roasts my potatoes. He had me thinking that all he watches are foreign language art films. Just wait until I see him."

Daisy squealed, "You can't say anything to him. Technically, we weren't supposed to be in his attic."

"Technically?! How about not in any way, shape or form were you supposed to be in his attic." Rose paced some more and huffed, "Well, now I don't know what to do. I really would love to give him a piece of my mind, but I can't think how I'd explain why my mother and sister happened to be sneaking around his shop."

Angela said, "Perhaps you could tell him we saw an intruder and went to investigate."

Rose plopped into a chair. "Right. Instead of calling the police, or even just calling Peter, you and Daisy slipped in through the attic window. Somehow, I don't think he'd believe it.

"Anyway," she sighed. "I don't know. Just a couple of hours

with that woman and I'm ready to climb the walls. The thought of living with her might make anyone turn to junk food and bad movies. I guess it's better than becoming an alcoholic." She took a large sip of her drink. "It's just so sad that he can't admit it."

Angela said, "Yes, it is sad. Aren't you girls pleased that you can tell me anything at all? I pass no judgment. It's a gift of mine. Why, you could drink this whole pitcher of Marauders and I wouldn't utter a word."

Daisy picked up the empty pitcher and said, "That's true, you wouldn't." She smiled at her mother, "Not unless we didn't leave any for you. Okay, ladies, time for bed. It's really late."

Rose yawned and said, "Thank God we don't have to get up in the morning." As they were trailing up the steps she asked Daisy, "Did he have any really good candy? Anything I'd like?"

"Ab-zo-lutely, as Rocky would say. Twizzlers and Good'n'Plenty."

"Okay, then. It's really all good, isn't it?"

The shop was closed on Sundays and Mondays, Daisy and Rose adamantly refusing to give in to the 24/7 school of doing business. So Sunday mornings were slow and easy.

They had just had their first cup of tea and Angela was fixing omelets when Bill Greene dropped by about noon to pick up the police file Elyse Dove had given them.

Daisy answered the door and said, "This is Sunday. I thought you were off duty."

"Technically, I am, but I need to get a handle on all this. So far, we've got a lot of nothing."

As they got to the kitchen Rose said, "Coffee? Tea?"

"I could use a cup of coffee. I've been up most of the night."

Rose put the coffee on and they sat at the table. Daisy asked, "Anything new on the investigation? Have you figured out what was used to kill Brad?"

"We know it was the same thing that killed Peggy Merritt,

but we're not sure what it is. Something round and flat, about three inches in diameter."

"Like a hammer?"

"We're not sure. The depression's kind of big for a hammer."

Rose suggested, "Maybe it's some specialty mallet."

"Could be. The techs are hammering away with everything from a metal crab mallet to a small sledgehammer trying to find something that leaves the same mark."

Angela asked, "Any forensics? DNA, hair follicles, clothing fibers? Was there petechial hemorrhaging? I always like the sound of that. Was there skin under his nails? Any defensive wounds?"

Bill shook his head and said, "You watch too much TV, Angela. No. We haven't found much at all actually. We do know that Brad wasn't killed where you found him. It looks like the murderer just dumped the body back there."

Rose asked, "Why? That's a lot of trouble to go to. I mean they really had to work to shove him behind the garage like that."

Daisy said, "And there was a huge chance they'd be seen. That's crazy."

Bill said, "Could be a number of reasons. Most obvious would be that wherever Douglas was murdered would clearly incriminate the murderer. Maybe he wanted to lay the blame on you two or just scare you silly. Or maybe he just wanted to hide the body hoping to obscure the time of death. Who knows?"

He finished his coffee and said, "Thanks. Have you got that file for me on the girl from Virginia?"

Daisy picked it up and handed it to him. "I hope it helps. I just know that baseball card is at the bottom of this mess. And I would love to find it and give it back to Elyse."

Bill took the file and said, "I'll let you know what I find out."

Daisy walked out with him to get the morning paper. She looked up at the clear, blue sky and sighed, "Oh wow, what a beautiful day. Mid-eighties and sunny. What a relief. I hope the whole week will be like this."

"Daisy, what planet do you live on? We have a hurricane headed this way. They think it's going to hit us late in the week."

"A hurricane! How did I miss that? I'll go check it out right now."

Angela was putting the omelets on the table when Daisy hurried back up the stairs. "Come on, honey, eat it while it's hot."

Daisy said, "Just a minute." She quickly scanned the newspaper and, sure enough, there was a picture of Hurricane Bathsheba heading toward the east coast - estimated landfall Thursday evening.

"How could I have missed this? Did either of you know about it?" she asked as she handed the paper to Rose.

Angela read over her daughter's shoulder and said, "I did hear something at the salon, but those ladies totally exaggerate everything, so I didn't pay attention."

They finished brunch and cleaned up. Then Rose got out a paper and pencil.

Daisy asked, "What are you doing?"

"I'm going to make a list of what we need to do before this thing hits. Thank God we're not in a flood zone, but we could lose electricity or have wind damage. We'd better be prepared."

Angela jumped up and cried "Hurricane party!"

Daisy said, "Not here, Mother. You're going home where it's safer." Angela lived in an upscale senior citizens community near Annapolis just half an hour's drive from Old Towne.

"Must I?"

"Yes, you must. They have backup generators and a whole staff working to make sure you're safe and you have what you need. Invite some friends over and have a hurricane party there."

Angela brightened. "You're right. I'll call the girls and we can all wear our pajamas. We'll have fun."

Rose had been jotting down her own list and said, "Sounds good to me. I wish we could come. Our list isn't nearly as much fun."

"I hope you put the wine and vodka on it, at least," said Daisy.

"Of course, I did. But we have a lot to do. The patio furniture has to be brought in, and I think we should tape the sunroom windows."

"Isn't that a tad excessive?"

"The paper says we could get a direct hit. Trees might come down and if something hit those windows that glass could be really dangerous."

Daisy asked, "How bad do you think it's going to be? Do you think we need to put away the crystal and glass in the shop?"

"Not really. I'm just worried about all that wall of glass."

"Well, now I am, too. Thanks a lot."

Around two Wednesday afternoon Rose was in the office when Tonya stuck her head in and said, "I'm running down the street to see if Mom and Dad need any help, if that's all right."

"Sure. Take your time. Daisy and I are fine here. In fact, I think we'll close up soon anyway. Take the rest of the day off."

"Thanks." She turned to go, but stopped, turned back to Rose and said, "What am I doing? I was going to walk out with this." She handed her a large brown envelope. "I found it on the floor under the counter. I don't know who left it or when."

"Rose took the envelope and said, "Thanks. Go help your parents. And don't come in tomorrow. I don't want you fighting your way home if this thing comes in earlier than expected."

Tonya left and Rose looked at the envelope. A cold feeling came over her. "Daisy, come here and look at this."

Daisy looked at the envelope and said, "What? It doesn't say anything."

"Exactly. Who leaves an envelope with no name on it?"

"Well, open it! It might not even be for us."

Rose carefully opened the envelope and pulled out a sheet of paper, looked at it and dropped it on the counter. The message was a cut and paste job. Rose said, "Short and to the point."

the card or your dead

"Rose! This is creepy," said Daisy.

"You got that right. I'm calling Bill now." As she dialed she said, "Who could have left this?"

Daisy said, "Anyone. This place has been Grand Central Station all week."

Rose said, "Bill's not answering. I'll have to leave a message." She listened for the beep, then said, "Bill, it's Rose. Call me as soon as you get this. We just got a letter from Brad's killer."

Chapter Twenty-Four

Rose put the phone down and said, "What do we do now?"

Daisy practically shouted, "How should I know? We don't even have the card. That bastard has it! He practically killed you getting it!"

"Daisy, calm down. We have to think this through. I just hope Bill calls back soon." She took a deep breath. "Okay. Apparently, the killer does not have the card. So where is it?"

"Could it possibly still be here?"

"How? Where? I checked. You checked. The envelope was gone right after the bastard attacked me. This makes no sense at all."

"Maybe it was Brad who attacked you and stole the card back."

"Well then, why didn't the killer find it? Why would he think we still had it?"

"I have no idea why anyone thinks anything anymore. I do know that I am not happy with this situation. The idiot didn't even tell how we are supposed to get the damned thing to him."

Rose sighed. "I know. If we could figure out when this note came, maybe we could narrow down who wrote it."

Daisy said, "It wasn't there on Monday. I swept the floor and dusted the entire counter. I would have seen it. But it's been so crazy anyone could have dropped it, pretty much any time after that.

"Rose, it's probably someone we know. It could be a friend. They've all been around this week; Peter, Marc, Mary, the neighbors, everybody. The only person I didn't see around this week was Jeff Moody."

"Jeff Moody? Somehow, I'd forgotten all about him. I guess I kind of ruled him out when we found out that he's the bobber. But really, Daisy, you could be right. He could easily be the blackmailer.

"And just because we didn't see him, doesn't mean he didn't drop off the envelope. He could have come by while we were out."

"What are we going to do?"

"First things first. We're not going to panic. We're going to get this place hurricane ready while we wait for Bill to call back."

Daisy looked at her sister for a long moment. "You're a very practical person. Did you know that?"

"Yes, I am. Getting hysterical doesn't help much. Right now, I think we should check on Ron and Sarah. See if they need any help. Then we should bring in everything we can from outside."

"You're right. It's getting late anyway. I'm putting the closed sign out and we'll go be good little neighbors. I just hope they aren't the little neighbors who want to kill us for a baseball card."

Rose found Ron Tucker packing up his car. He was leaving to stay at his daughter's for a few days. "Everything's put away. I think we're all making a big deal out of nothing, but my Lindy is having fits. She won't rest if I stay here alone."

"I don't blame her. I hope you're right and this is all wasted effort, but we really do need to be ready for the worst," said Rose.

"Will you girls be all right here alone?"

"We'll be fine. We've got plenty of food and batteries. We'll see you in a few days."

She met Daisy coming back from Mrs. Hudson's. "She and

Abby are off to Abby's parents' house."

"Good. Let's go over to the Tavern and get something to eat. We'll see what Mattie and Frank are planning to do."

"Sounds good. Has Bill called back yet?"

"No. I'll try him again when we get home."

They were dragging in the last of the lawn furniture inside when Bill finally called back. "Read the letter to me."

Rose read the note. "He didn't include delivery instructions." There was silence on the end of the line. "Bill, you there?"

"Yes. I'm thinking. You and Daisy can't stay there. You need to leave. I can't get over there right now. I'm up to my ears with preparation for this storm and I need you and Daisy someplace safe."

"We're safe. We've got the alarm and the dog. We'll check everything twice. Besides, where would we go?"

"Just go to your mother's for a couple of days."

"I don't think so. Daisy, me, Mother, two dogs, a cat and mother's pals in a small townhouse? Not going to happen."

"How about your boyfriend?"

"We're not that friendly."

"Well then, what about Marc what's-his-name? Daisy's friend?"

"Again, not that friendly, and he lives near the water. He's probably worried about flooding. Really, Bill, we'll be fine."

"I don't like it. You're sitting ducks there alone. You could stay at my place."

"With Bambi? That would be rich. No, we're staying here. We'll keep in touch with you and Tom Willis. I'll talk to you tomorrow."

Daisy had been listening to the conversation.

"That moron didn't really suggest you and I should spend a few days with that frizzy-haired wacko, did he? We'd kill each other and you'd have to referee."

"He's worried about us. And so am I, really. I know I keep saying we'll be fine, but will we? We are going to be totally alone here. The Tavern is closing, the neighbors are gone. It's just you and me."

Daisy smiled and said, "I'm not worried. I plan on drinking my way through this thing. I've got all the makings for Hurricanes and corned beef sandwiches. I've got two coolers filled with ice, in case we lose electricity, and we have the Bunsen burner for hot water in the morning. What else could we possibly need? We will be fine."

"It's not so much the storm I'm worried about."

"I know. But nobody is going to come out in this mess. He'd have to be crazy."

"Maybe he is."

Thursday morning the rain started to come in. In the afternoon the wind picked up. Malcolm and Roscoe were unhappy. They paced and howled. Daisy and Rose called Angela on speaker phone to make sure she was all right.

"I'm wonderful. The girls are here and we're snug as bugs in rugs. I wish you two would come over. You still have time. I have a bad feeling. Something's going to happen and I won't be able to help."

"Mom, nothing is going to happen. It's just this weather. It's depressing. And you already have a houseful. Just relax. You and the ladies have fun."

"Oh, we will. But you two sleep downstairs. I don't want a tree coming down on you."

"We already planned to do just that. We love you, Mom. We'll talk tomorrow."

"I love you, too. Take care."

They hung up. Daisy made lunch. They watched the weather on TV. Bathsheba had been downgraded to a Category 1 and was coming in a little to the east. So, not a direct hit, but bad enough.

Later that afternoon, Rose handed Daisy a cocktail and they

settled on the couch to wait it out. She asked, "Have you checked the doors and windows?"

"Yes. Twice. Everything is locked and bolted. Shades are down, curtains closed. Alarm on. Animals inside. Drink up! We've done all we can."

"I know. But when Mother has a bad feeling, I don't like to ignore it."

And so they sat and listened to the wind shrieking through the trees, the rain beating against the side of the house, and the sound of sirens in the distance. It was six o'clock and the hurricane was beginning to descend on them with its full force.

They slipped in a movie and made popcorn and wondered how long they would have electricity.

Angela was having fun. It was ten o'clock and the wind hadn't let up for hours. The lights had flickered a few times causing everyone to scream. But the four friends were safe and as comfortable as they could be.

They were playing Pictionary and drinking Angela's *Naked Runner* cocktails. Angela's best friend, Regina Owens, wearing pink baby-doll PJs that barely covered her more than ample rear end, was drawing for her team. When she dropped her marker and bent over to pick it up, someone shouted, "We need a picture!"

She stood up abruptly and said, "No, you don't."

But Angela pulled out her camera and said, "Come on ladies. Smile for the camera. We need to make a record for posterity."

She got pictures of everyone and a really nice group shot of the four of them huddled together in front of the picture window using the ten second delay.

Regina said, "You can't see the storm, you know."

"I know, but we'll remember it. I'm putting these on the computer right now. We'll email them to our kids."

"Oh lord, my kids already think I'm nuts."

There was a knock on the door and Angela opened it to one of the community's security guards. He took one look at the four women and turned bright red. Regina was, of course, wearing the pink baby-dolls. The other two women, Theresa and Dot were wearing nightshirts. Theresa's had a voluptuous bikini-clad woman's body on it giving the impression that it was her own. Dot's had a picture of Georgia O'Keeffe's sexually suggestive *Black Iris* with the inscription 'You should see *MY* iris!' And Angela was wearing a pale green, very short, chiffon dress with gold braid crisscrossing the bodice, and fairy wings. She was also wearing a miner's light on her head.

Angela asked, "Is there a problem?"

"No." He looked at her strangely. "I'm sorry. I didn't mean to interrupt anything."

"Oh, you're not. We're having a little pajama party to wait out the hurricane." She looked at her friends and laughed. "I guess we do look a little odd."

Dot, who was pouring another round, said, "*You* look a little odd, dear."

"I do? Oh, well, yes, I guess the miner's light looks a bit silly. But if we lose power, you'll thank me."

"No, sweetie. Not the miner's light."

Angela looked down at her outfit and whispered to the poor guy, "I see. These are not really pajamas. Just between you, me and my headlight, I don't wear nighties in the summer. So I just pulled out this little number I wore for Halloween a few years ago. I was a fairy."

The poor guy simply didn't know what to say to that. He cleared his throat and finally croaked, "I'm just checking on everyone and I noticed your drapes were open. You should probably close them. We don't want anything flying through the glass."

"I certainly will. Can you come in for a little drinkie-poo?"

"Thanks, but I'm on duty."

"Of course you are. Well, don't get blown away." She smiled as she closed the door and said, "What a nice boy."

The ladies got back to the game while Angela uploaded the pictures. She was giggling as she looked through them. "These are great. Our kids will love them!"

When she came to the group shot she called over her shoulder, "This is really good. We look wonderful." But as she stared at it, something bothered her. Something was off balance.

Then she laughed. Of course, there it was in the corner of the shot. She could just make out the security guard's face as he passed by the window under the porch light. It was kind of spooky looking. Then she stopped laughing, put her hand to her mouth, and whispered, "Oh, no. Oh no. Oh no. That's what was wrong."

She quickly opened the email from Daisy with the pictures Elyse Dove had given them. She flipped through to the shot of Margaret and her friends that had seemed so off to her before.

Angela enlarged the picture, so she could see everything in the background. She grabbed the phone and dialed Rose's cell. No answer. She tried Daisy's, but it went straight to voicemail. Next she tried their landline. It rang, then she heard crackling on the line, then silence.

She was getting frantic. She thought for a minute and then called the Bostwick police station and asked for Tom Willis. She waited and finally heard his voice saying, "I'm currently out of the office. Please leave a message and I'll get back to you as soon as possible."

"Tom, you need to call me right now. I've just seen the killer!"

Chapter Twenty-Five

Daisy's cell rang and she nearly jumped out of her skin. She grabbed it and said, "Hello? Hello? Who is this?"

"Daisy? It's Marc. Are you all right?"

It was a bit past ten o'clock and the storm was really going to town. She and Rose had tried to watch a movie, but the wind and rain were now so loud, they couldn't concentrate.

"Marc? Oh, sorry. I'm a little on edge. The phones haven't been working and it startled me when it rang. Is everything okay there?"

"Sure. I'm just watching the water creep up the lawn. I wanted to check on you and Rose. Not that I could do anything much really."

"That's a kind thought, Marc. We're okay. I'm just jumpy. Marc? Marc?" She put the phone down. "We got cut off."

"The circuits are overloaded. When Peter called earlier, he said he had tried for over an hour before he got through and then we got cut off, too. Have another drink. You need to relax."

"I know I do. That wind just sounds so sinister. It's unnerving."

Rose yawned and said, "At least we have electricity. You know what? I'm going to take a shower while it's still on. Then maybe we can get a little sleep."

"You're going to take a shower? Upstairs? In this?"

"In what? It's not raining in here. I'll just be a couple of minutes."

Rose grabbed a flashlight and ran up the stairs. A minute later

Daisy heard the water running. She put Roscoe on her lap and rubbed his ears. "I hate this storm." Roscoe butted her chin with his head as if agreeing totally that this storm wasn't his cup of tea either.

Suddenly the wind stopped howling. At the same time the landline rang sounding like a fire alarm in the eerie silence. Daisy jumped up knocking the cat to the floor and tripping over Malcolm who was curled up at her feet.

Daisy grabbed the phone and said, "Hello?"

A pathetic sounding voice said, "Help. Please. I'm alone. Can you come get me?"

"Who is this? I can hardly hear you." The wind started shrieking again and Daisy had to strain to hear. "Who is this?"

"This is Mrs. Hudson. Is that Daisy? Can you help me?"

"Mrs. Hudson? Where are you?"

"I'm next door, dear. I decided to stay. But something just fell outside and I'm scared. Can you and Rose come and get me?"

"Oh my God, yes. I'm on my way. Get your boots and raincoat on. I'll hurry." She hung up the phone and ran up the stairs. She shouted into the bathroom, "Rose, Mrs. Hudson is stuck in her house. I'm running over there to get her."

Rose called out, "What did you say?"

Daisy yelled back as she was in her closet digging out her old boots, "I'm going next door to rescue Mrs. Hudson. We'll be back in a couple of minutes."

Rose turned off the water and heard Daisy running down the stairs. "Wait a minute. Where are you going? I'll come with you. Daisy, wait for me." But Daisy was already gone.

Rose hurriedly dried off and pulled on shorts and a tee shirt. As she was leaving her room, the phone rang. She grabbed it and shouted, "What?" She thought she heard her mother's voice for just a second, but the line went dead.

She hung up, picked the receiver up again and listened for a dial tone. Nothing. A dreadful feeling crept over her as she put the phone back down. She grabbed her flashlight and went downstairs calling out to her sister.

Daisy wasn't there. Malcolm and Roscoe were huddled on the couch. Roscoe's hair was on end. Rose asked, "What's wrong with you guys? And where did that half-wit sister of mine go?"

A soft voice whispered in her ear, "She went next door to save that half-wit old lady. You should have gone too."

Daisy ran down the steps to the back door, put on her slicker and pulled the hood up. Then she turned off the alarm and opened the back door. She slammed it again murmuring to herself, "Front door, idiot!"

She ran back up the steps, through the living room, then down the front steps and out the door. She was almost knocked down by the first gust of wind she encountered and had to walk doubled over down the sidewalk. As she got to the Hudson house, she looked up. No lights were on.

She looked back at her own house. Still lit up, so the power was on. She got to the front porch and banged on the door. "Mrs. Hudson, it's Daisy."

The door swung open and Daisy stepped inside. She called out again, "Mrs. Hudson? Sarah? Where are you? Are you all right? Why are your lights off?" She fumbled for the light switch and turned it on. Sarah Hudson was sitting a chair in her chartreuse robe and fuzzy, turquoise slippers, tears running down her face.

She looked at Daisy with sad, terrified eyes and said, "Where's Rose? You were both supposed to come."

"Mrs. Hudson, what's going on? You're not even dressed. Why was Rose supposed to come?"

Daisy stared at the old woman, her gaze drawn to the fuzzy slippers on her feet. And then she pictured Rose standing in the water on their back porch holding up her "clue" – a piece of blue fuzz.

"It was you? You tried to flood our house? Why?"

The old lady just looked at her.

Daisy grabbed her arm and shouted, "Mrs. Hudson! What the hell is going on?"

Sarah Hudson sighed and finally said, "You couldn't just leave well enough alone. If you'd just gotten rid of that card, it would all be okay. I was trying to warn you off. But it's too late. Sit down and have a cup of tea. You're going to need it."

A cold sensation rushed over Daisy. She hesitated a moment, then ran out the door and fought her way back up the street. She paused in front of the house and looked up into the living room window. She saw the shadow of two people struggling with each other. She screamed and started running up the walk. At that moment all of the lights went out.

Rose dropped her flashlight, as a strong arm wrapped around her neck. In the mirror over the couch she saw Abby Wentworth in a black rain slicker holding a five-pound dumbbell over her head.

Abby hissed, "Where is it? That card, I need it now. I need to get away from here and I'm running out of time."

"I don't have it. You've got it. Remember. We've done this before."

"That envelope was empty. There was no card in it."

"Well, I can't help it if you lost it."

Abby shrieked into Rose's ear, "I want the card now!"

Rose was thinking frantically. "Brad must have stolen it back before you got here the last time. That must have been the card in the frame in his shop."

"Wrong! Wrong, wrong, wrong!" She was screaming. "That was a copy, a freaking color copy. Now tell me where you hid the damned card or I will bring this weight down on your ugly head!"

"I can't tell you what I don't know. I don't have the baseball card."

Abby raised her arm to strike, but Rose jerked sideways and the weight came down hard on her shoulder. She screamed in pain, but managed to bite the arm around her neck and break free. She fell hard to the floor and was scrambling frantically trying to reach her heavy flashlight, as she felt Abby straddle her legs. Then the maniac started swinging the dumbbell like a hammer. Rose rolled to her left and then to her right as the weight came down again and again missing her by inches with each swing.

As Abby's arm came down a third time, Rose managed to throw herself over it and pin it under her, but she had no leverage. Abby pulled her arm free and was raising the dumbbell for a final deadly attack when everything went black. Rose rolled away as far as she could. She braced herself for the blow, covering her head with her arms. But instead of pain, she felt Abby roll off her legs and heard her start screaming in terror. Then Rose heard the weight fall to the floor.

Suddenly, there was pounding on the stairs and Daisy ran in shouting, "Oh my God, Rose. Where are you? Are you all right?"

Daisy shone her light across the room. Rose shouted over Abby's screams, "Over here. Shine it over here." Daisy spotted her and Rose found her own flashlight, turned it on, and jumped to her feet.

They both moved their lights to the center of the room where Abby Wentworth lay on the floor, crying now, and pleading for them to help her. The dumbbell lay near her, but she was covering her face with both hands. Roscoe was perched on her head, his claws embedded in her scalp. Malcolm sat placidly on the middle of her back, a chunk of red hair hanging out of his mouth.

An hour later, in the glow of the candlelit room, Daisy and Rose were sprawled on the couch drinks in hand, a pitcher of Hurricanes sitting on the table, and an ice pack on Rose's shoulder. Mrs. Hudson sat at the dining room table in a slightly damp robe sipping a glass of water. On the far side of the living room sat Abby Wentworth; hair wild, hands, feet and torso duct-taped to a chair. Roscoe was sitting on a small table to her left, as still as stone, his gaze never leaving her face. Malcolm sat at attention on her right. She looked absolutely terrified.

Rose turned on an old cassette player she had dug out of the closet and said, "I knew this would come in handy someday. Okay, where shall we start? Murder? Blackmail? Ah Mrs. H. Good."

Mrs. Hudson said, "I feel like this is all my fault, but you have to understand. I was having trouble making ends meet. And then I remembered these old stories about Mattie and Sally. And thought what could it hurt really? They had so much, they wouldn't miss a little here and there. So I wrote them a note and they paid up."

"Why didn't you just ask them for help? Or us? We'd have been happy to help you out."

"And take charity? I could never take charity."

Daisy's mouth fell open. "But you could take blackmail? Wow." She got up to refill her glass. "How did little Abby get into the picture?"

"A couple of summers ago when she was staying with me she found the ledger where I keep track of everything."

Abby hissed, "Shut up you fool! Don't say another word." Malcolm growled softly and she closed her mouth.

Sarah didn't look at her niece, she just continued her story. "Abby took over and threatened to turn me in to the police if I tried to stop her. I was so afraid I looked the other way."

Abby said, "You've forgotten to mention the money I was

giving you."

Rose cried, "Mrs. Hudson!" A gust of wind rattled the house and they heard a deafening thud as a tree fell somewhere in the neighborhood. "Abby, why don't you keep the story going? I want to get this on tape before a tree comes through the roof."

Abby glared at them. "You're crazy. I'm not saying a word." Roscoe hissed and moved closer to her face. "Get him away from me."

"Tell us what happened and we will," said Daisy. "Who's Charlie Taylor?"

Abby was silent. Mrs. Hudson said, "She is. Abigail Charles Wentworth Taylor. She was married for a short time and used her old identification to set up the mail boxes."

Abby screamed, "Aunt Sarah, shut up!"

"Or what, dear. You'll murder me like you did that woman in the post office?"

Rose's voice was consoling as she said, "Abby, we already have you for trying to kill me. And Malcolm is really angry about that. I'd hate to see what he'd do if I let him."

Malcolm snarled and bared his teeth. Abby yelled, "All right." She stretched as much as she could backing away from the animals. "All right. That bitch dying was a mistake. I guess you already figured out that your post office box is right next to mine. I had already gotten a day's worth of your mail. I figured maybe the old bat had put Brad's card in your box instead of mine. She showed up just as I got the door and I hit her with my dumb bell. It was only two pounds. I didn't mean to kill her."

Rose looked at the dumbbell on the floor and said, "Five pounds? I guess this time you meant business." Malcolm growled. "Good boy Malcolm. Stay close. But we've gotten a little ahead of ourselves. Daisy and I, and the police actually, already know that the card belonged to a girl named Margaret Dove and that she died on the Outer Banks in 2008. How did Brad get the card?"

"He stole it from her. How else? Brad and I have known each other since high school. I was with him when he met her at the card show. Of course, he knew right away what that card was worth."

Rose held up a finger. "Hold it a second." She poured herself another drink, checked the tape recorder, and said, "Okay, keep going. Did you kill that poor girl?"

"No!" Roscoe hissed and batted her arm with his paw. Abby shrieked, but Rose asked, "Did Brad?"

"Not exactly. He just didn't help her. I'm pretty sure he was planning to steal the card when he asked her out. They were walking on the beach and she fell into a hole and hit her head. Some idiot had left a cinderblock in it. She was unconscious."

"Why didn't he pick her up or call for help?"

"He did. He called me. I met him on the pier and I told him we had to go get her. By the time we got back to where he left her, the tide had come in. It was a huge surf that night and the beach was covered. She was gone. I told him to call the police and then I left. I didn't see Brad again until he showed up here. When he showed everyone that card, I pretended not to remember it. But I knew he must have taken it from her that night. And I thought, 'Here's my ticket out.' And if that bitch in the post office hadn't screwed up I'd be in California right now!"

"He must have known you were the blackmailer."

She laughed. "Brad was never the fastest pitcher on the mound. And I think he loved me."

Rose shook her head. "Last question. Why in heaven's name did you kill him?"

"Because he was a freaking moron. After I broke in here..." Roscoe hissed and she cringed, but went on, "I thought I had the card, but the envelope was empty. I knew the card in the frame was a fake..."

Daisy said, "Because of the color."

"Yeah. Well, I thought he was trying to hide it from me, but then he asks me to meet him by that big old tree in your yard. The idiot still didn't know I was the one who was blackmailing him. He tells me everything and asks what he should do." She started laughing hysterically, then burst out in tears.

In between sobs and laughter she managed to get out, "I told him he should give it to me. When I realized he really didn't have it, I got mad and hit him in the head."

The sound of the tape whirring in the machine stopped abruptly and it clicked off. Rose said, "Perfect timing."

They heard banging on the front door. Rose started to get up to answer it, but Daisy said, "Don't bother. I didn't lock it. They can just come on up."

Rose fell back onto the couch and put the ice pack back on her shoulder. "Okeydokey."

In a minute Bill Greene, followed by Tom Willis, came stomping up the stairs shouting, "Why is your door open?"

The two men stopped short when they came through the door. Bill said, "What the...?"

Daisy said, "The friendly neighborhood murderer was already here, so I didn't feel the need to lock the door. Nice of you to drop by. How's the storm? Care for a drink?" She lifted the pitcher and realized it was empty. "Oops, I think we need another."

Bill said, "You're drunk!"

Daisy looked at Mrs. Hudson and said, "He's an excellent detective."

Bill said, "Daisy, I think you should sit down. Why is that woman taped to a chair?"

Daisy turned and looked him in the eye and said, "Bill, Bill, Bill. First things first. We need a bit more rum." She turned to her sister, "Don't we, Rose?"

"Yes we do. Come on guys, sit down. Daisy makes a damned good cocktail. It's usually my job, but my shoulder is killing me." She looked at Abby and tittered, "Ha! No it's not. It is not killing me. So there, you little freak."

Abby started to say something, but Rose put her finger to her lips and shook her head. "No more talking. It's all right here." She tapped the recorder with her toe. Malcolm barked and Abby stayed quiet.

Rose managed to sit up straight. "Bill, Abby was trying to hammer my head with that weight on the floor over there. We thought that was a very bad idea, so we taped her to the chair."

Daisy came back in with another pitcher. She reeled a bit as she walked past Tom and he caught the pitcher just before she dumped it all over him.

Bill was clearly exasperated. "Could someone tell me what's going on here? Your mother's calling everyone in town and leaving messages saying she knows Abby did it and you're not safe."

"You got a call? Heck, we only got a text message I still don't know what it says. Here, look at this." Daisy handed Tom her phone. "See. 'Abby is JILLDR. She IZ?KN PICGJFRR AITH Magrt DO E. GE LLOK.' Could you make sense of that? I ask you."

Rose chimed in, "Of course, by the time we got the message, we already guessed that our little Abby wasn't such a nice person."

Abby started crying, "Billy, help me. They're crazy. They sicced their freaky animals on me and then they attacked me and taped me to this chair. And Daisy dragged my poor aunt over here through all the rain and wind."

Roscoe hissed, Malcolm bared his teeth, and Daisy and Rose both said, "Oh shut up!" at the same time. Abby shut up. Then Rose continued, "Billy, now let me introduce Charlie Taylor, blackmailer extraordinaire. And duct taper of little dogs. And, of course, the big one-murderer of various people."

"Tom, please, make them let me go. Get these monsters away from me. I'm begging you." Abby sounded so pitiful that Tom

Willis moved to help her.

Mrs. Hudson spoke up softly. She sounded tired and sad. "I wouldn't do that Officer. She's really very dangerous."

Daisy held out a cassette recorder and handed it to Bill. "It's all on there. Well, most of it. A fairly complete confession. Seems little Miss All-American, Mom and apple pie here is absolutely terrified of our little furry friends. One little look and she couldn't stop talking."

Bill took the cassette and turned it on. Abby's voice came on answering question after question from Rose and Daisy. He listened for a minute, then turned it off and Abby started sobbing. "None of that is true. I was so scared I just said what I thought they wanted me to."

Once again, Mrs. Hudson spoke. She didn't get up, or look at them. "I'm so ashamed. I started this whole thing. I'm a weak, horrible person. But I can tell both of you that every word on that tape is the truth. I'll swear to it."

Abby screamed, "You bitch! You nasty, creepy, old woman! No wonder the family can't find anyone to take care of you."

She pointed at her aunt with her nose. "She's the blackmailer. She's been doing it for years. Arrest her." Her face was so contorted with rage that Malcolm shrank back. But Roscoe moved closer to her, hissing, his back arched and hair on end. She started screaming hysterically.

"Daisy, move the damned cat. And the dog. Abby's not going anywhere."

"Oh, okay." Daisy picked up Roscoe and said, "That's my good little guy." She patted Malcolm on the head, "You, too. Come to the kitchen and we'll have some shrimp."

Abby stopped screaming. She sat there looking at Rose with sheer venom in her eyes, but she kept her mouth shut.

Bill was silent for a minute. He turned to Tom Willis. "Watch them. I'm going to listen to this and try to figure out what to do." He sat across from Mrs. Hudson at the dining room table, put the ear phones in, and listened.

Half an hour later he turned off the machine. He moved over to Abby, took out a pen knife and cut away the tape. She smiled wickedly at Rose and Daisy and was just reaching up to give Bill a hug when he pulled out his handcuffs and said, "Abigail Wentworth, also known as Charlie Taylor, I'm arresting you on suspicion of the murders of Peggy Merritt and Brad Douglas." And then he proceeded to read her Miranda rights.

Chapter Twenty-Six

Daisy stumbled down the steps into the kitchen. Sun was streaming through the windows and she could hear power saws already at work in the neighborhood. She looked into the living room and saw Rose on the couch where she had left her the night before. Malcolm, snuggled up beside her, lifted his head inquiringly.

Roscoe was weaving through her legs seeming to decide if he needed to go out more than he wanted to eat. Daisy picked him up and took him down to the back door and let him into the yard. Malcolm heard them and came tearing down the steps, almost knocking Daisy over to get outside.

She stepped onto the porch and marveled at the gorgeous day. It was hard to believe it was such a nightmare just hours before. The sky was a robin's egg blue filled with huge, fluffy white cumulus clouds hanging so low she felt like she could touch them. The air was soft and balmy, only a light breeze drifted though the treetops.

As she stood on the porch, she surveyed the storm damage. No trees down, but a lot of debris scattered over the yard. And a good sized limb had knocked part of the fence down.

Next door, a large oak had smashed through Mrs. Hudson's roof. "Too bad," she thought. She called to the pets, "Holler when you want to come in. I've got tuna."

She wearily plodded back up the stairs and found Rose lighting the Bunsen burner. "Do you have any idea what time it is? The electric's still out. I'm making tea."

Daisy looked at her watch. "Almost eleven. I think I'll have a Pepsi, actually. And some aspirin. How's your shoulder?"

"Sore. Everything is sore. Remember when we were little and had our first ballet lesson and we could hardly walk for the next week? Well, this is worse. Every muscle in my body hurts."

Daisy handed Rose the aspirin, then busied herself getting food ready for the critters. "It's absolutely beautiful outside. Amazing!"

"How's the yard?"

"Not too bad. A bit of work to do with the fence. Some clean up. That tree we heard went through Sarah Hudson's roof."

"Huh. Where did Bill take her, anyway?"

"I'm not sure. I kind of lost track after that second pitcher. Next time I'll be more restrained."

Rose said, "Next time? No next time. I think we've had our fair share of murdering loonies, don't you?"

"Speaking of loonies…"

"Helloo-oo." The front door had opened and they heard Angela's voice call, "It took forever to get here, but I was so worried and your phones still aren't working. Tom got through to me this morning and told me what happened. He said you were all right, but I needed to see for myself." She got to the landing and pulled off her matching daisy print slicker and Wellington boots. "Muddy, everything is quite muddy!"

Roscoe and Malcolm scampered in behind her tracking mud through the apartment and made a beeline for their dishes. Percy brought up the rear, smiling his goofy doggie smile, obviously hoping for a dish of his own.

Angela walked into the dining room carrying a large bag and a thermos. She surveyed her daughters. "Hmm. I can see you've had a night. Tell me all."

She put the bag on the table and said, "But first things first." In a moment she had arranged a platter of fresh melon, grapes and nectarines next to another of delicate pastries. Out of the thermos came the fragrant aroma of cool mint tea. "You look as if you need rehydration, ladies. Lots of watermelon."

Rose breathed in deeply and said, "Heaven." They ate quietly for a few minutes until Angela finally said, "So, was I right? Was it really Abby?"

"You were right. How did you figure it out?"

"I told you in the text!"

"Mother, we couldn't read your text. Your typing is rotten. And, anyway, the message didn't come through until after we'd taped her up."

"Oh my goodness. Well, it was the picture of Margaret Dove with her friends. I told you, something bothered me about that picture from the first time I saw it.

"So last night I enlarged it on the computer and saw that there was another couple standing in the background, hardly visible. It was Abby, I could tell by the red hair, and Brad Douglas. And they seemed to be looking right at Margaret – like they knew her."

"They did. Not Margaret. Each other. They knew each other from a long time ago," said Rose. "And Brad was the man Margaret met in Nagshead. Roscoe got the whole story out of her. He's an amazing interrogator. All he had to do was hiss and it all came spilling out. And we were smart enough to tape it."

"Well, I want to know everything."

Daisy said, "Let's see. Where to begin? How about BLT#1 – Sarah 'I'm-just-a-sweet-old-lady' Hudson. She's a real winner!"

Rose recounted Mrs. Hudson's role in the whole mess.

Angela shook her head. "Why couldn't she just live on credit cards, like a good little American? Well, go on. I want to hear every last lurid detail."

Daisy said, "Okeydokey."

Rose got up to find ice for her shoulder. Angela asked, "What's wrong with your shoulder? Do you need to see a doctor?"

Rose winced, "No. It's just sore. We'll get to that lurid detail in a minute."

When they'd finished telling her about Margaret Dove's disappearance Angela shook her head, "The whole story sounds fishy. Do you think they planned to kill her together?"

Daisy said, "You know, I don't. I'm not sure how much to believe, but I do believe Margaret's death was unintended."

Rose got up and went to the window. She looked out at the bright sky and sighed, "I think you're right. Abby was definitely a schemer. And I'm sure she and/or Brad were planning on stealing the card. But I don't think they had murder in mind."

Daisy said, "And I'm guessing that Abby didn't think Brad had already stolen it. The next day everyone on the island was looking for the missing girl, but no one mentioned anything about a theft connected to it. So Abby just got out of there as fast as she could."

Angela put her pastry down. "What horrible people. To leave that poor girl there, on the beach alone!"

"He'd just stolen the baseball card from her. The really stupid aspect of the whole horrible mess was that he couldn't sell it. It's not like there are a ton of signed and dated Mantle rookie cards floating around out there. Someone would ask how he got it."

Angela said, "Well, accident or not, Brad Douglas was responsible for her death. They both were."

Daisy jumped up, "You know what? We need to get out of here. Let's take a walk. We can see what damage the storm did."

The girls ran upstairs, washed their faces and pulled on shorts, tee shirts, and flip-flops. Daisy took a minute to swipe on lip gloss and mascara. "No sense in scaring people. The storm's done enough of that."

Angela, in her Wellies, white Capri pants and blue sailor top, was waiting by the front door with the dogs. Daisy looked at Roscoe sitting on the landing and asked, "Are you coming, too?" He looked up at her a moment, squinted his eyes, and then padded back to the living room.

They walked toward the bike trail stepping over downed limbs and debris. Daisy and Rose skirted the large puddles. But Angela stomped right through each one, her eyes lighting up and smiling, saying, "You should have worn your boots."

Rose said, "Not as much damage as I thought there would be. It sounded much worse."

"It certainly could have been for us," said Daisy. She rubbed Malcolm's head. "But Malcolm and Roscoe took care of that nasty lady. Good boy. He's such a good boy!" Malcolm wagged his tail and took off after Percy.

Angela asked, "So, did Abby really kill the post office woman? Why?"

As they walked they told Angela the rest of the story. When they had finished Angela hugged Rose fiercely. "I am so glad you're okay. What would I do without you? What a truly horrid person!"

Rose said, "That she is."

Daisy called to the dogs, "Come back here. Time to go home." They came running back and took the lead as they all headed home.

The street was full of activity when they got there. Shop owners were checking for damage and a few insurance adjusters were already checking out the losses. But no reporters were hanging around and no one asked them about Abby or Sarah Hudson.

Daisy shook her head and said, "I don't know how Bill kept this quiet. I guess the storm helped."

Rose opened the door and trudged up the stairs. "I'm just glad he did. I am not up to answering a lot of questions right now."

Angela slipped off her boots and looked down at the muddy spots on her capris. "How did that happen?"

"Mother, you were jumping in puddles."

She smiled. "So I was. Well, just one last query - where is

this infamous baseball card?"

Rose said, "That is the question. We know Abby stole the envelope the card was in, but she swears up and down that it was empty when she got it home."

Daisy said, "It couldn't have been. I saw you put the card back into that envelope."

"And I put it on my dresser. Then I thought maybe I should hide it, so I stuck it in my sock drawer."

Daisy said, "Well, it must have slipped out of the envelope."

"I've looked everywhere. Everyone has. It's not here."

There was stomping on the stairs and Bill shouted, "You have to start locking your doors!"

Rose called out, "We figured you were coming."

He walked into the room and leaned against the doorjamb. "What's going on? You getting your stories straight?"

Daisy snorted and said, "Our stories are always straight. Besides, this time we are totally in the clear."

"Right! Then what did you do with this damned baseball card? Sorry, Angela, I'm tired." He looked at Daisy. "And don't do that thing with your eyes. You know I hate it."

Daisy was looking at him, squinting her eyes and pursing her lips. "We didn't do anything with the freaking card. We were just saying to Mother, we have no idea where it is. We don't have it. Apparently Abby doesn't. I can only think that Brad must have gotten it back somehow."

"Nope, he didn't." He looked tired and frustrated.

Rose asked, "Are you okay? You look terrible."

"Thanks. It's been a long night and your little friend, Abby, isn't exactly a charmer. But she swears Brad didn't have the thing. She says he thought she did. Her new story is he came after her and she just defended herself."

"I'll bet," said Daisy. "That's not what she told us and, besides, somehow I can't see Brad being a match for little Miss Sunshine."

Bill sat down suddenly in the arm chair, ran his hands over his face, and yawned. Rose asked, "Can I get you something? Soda? Water? Bourbon? We don't have anything hot."

"A soda would be good. Thanks."

They waited until Rose came back with a tray of drinks, corned beef, rye bread, and potato salad. "Eat. We need to finish all of this before the ice in the cooler melts. Besides, you look like you could use something to eat."

Bill said, "You're right. I could. I haven't eaten anything since the storm began," as he made himself a large sandwich.

Rose asked, "What about Mrs. Hudson? What's going to happen to her?"

"Good question. Right now, she's out on bond. At her age if she co-operates and testifies against Abby she'll probably get probation. As for her own little blackmail racket, nobody has pressed charges. As far as the police know, there was no blackmail."

"What about the doghouse fire and the flood?"

"Only if you want to charge her. Then we'd have to prove she did it."

Daisy sighed, "What would be the use?"

Rose said, "That fire could have done some terrible damage. So could the flood."

Angela said, "And I'm not sure I'll ever get over seeing little Roscoe hanging from that tree!"

They looked at each other. Finally Daisy said, "We won't press charges. She'll have enough problems with the house and Abby. Everybody around here will know most of it in a few days, anyway. And she'll have to live with that."

Angela nodded her head. "I think that's best. And now there is just one big question left - who has that card? I really wanted to return it to Elyse Dove. It means so much to her."

Bill got up to leave. "That I don't know. If you figure it out, you'd better tell me. I hate loose ends. Speaking of which, Willis thought you'd like to know that that naked guy was picked up last night. He was actually out in the storm."

Saturday morning the electricity came back on and everyone was out with chainsaws, shovels and rakes. The only outstanding damage was the tree through Mrs. Hudson's roof.

Rose was in the garden working on the poor zinnia bed once again when Ron Tucker dropped by. "I just heard about Abby and all the trouble you had during the storm the other night. I can't believe it. She seemed like such a nice girl."

Rose said, "I know. I guess you can't tell about people, can you? Who did you talk to? Or is the story in the newspaper?"

"I got it from Sarah. I've been trying to call her since I got back and saw that hole in her roof. I finally tracked her down at her sister's place. She's in a real state. She told me Abby's in jail because she killed that woman from the post office and the Brad fella. She wasn't making a lot of sense and I don't think she's coming back. What in blazes went on here?"

Rose said, "Ron, it's a long story. Come in and have some iced tea and I'll tell you about it."

Ron, Rose and Daisy sat at the kitchen table for a long time and they told him the whole story leaving out Mattie and Sally's names. Ron just kept shaking his head and saying, "I'll be."

Then Daisy admitted that they had wondered if he might be the blackmailer for just a minute or two.

"Me? Why would you think that?"

"Because of Rex Harrison. Ron, you've never had a purebred dog in your life. And suddenly you had the cutest little pedigreed puppy. I'm really sorry and it's absolutely none of our business, but we just wondered how you could afford it."

Ron laughed and said, "Oh boy, I'll just bet you did wonder. He was a gift from Shirley Miles. She's my vet. Some lady dropped off three little puppies at her clinic and says she doesn't want them. Shirley thought of me. I got my pick."

By ten o'clock that evening the sisters were exhausted. They sat on the couch for a while until Daisy started nodding off. She jerked awake and said, "I'm off to bed. You coming, Rose?"

"In a while. As tired as I am, I think I'm too keyed up to sleep. See you in the morning."

Rose checked all the doors and turned on the alarm. Then she made herself a cup of tea and stood looking out of the living room window. Malcolm was sleeping on the couch, but sat up when he heard her sigh. "Sorry, little guy. I didn't want to wake you. I just wish I knew where that baseball card is. It's making me crazy." She rubbed his head and walked up to her bedroom.

She got into bed and picked up the book on the night table. It was the book Angela had borrowed, *Murder Gets a Life*. Rose opened it and began to read. After half an hour she yawned and slipped the bookmark Angela had left in it into place, closed the book, and turned off the light.

She was almost asleep when she sat up suddenly, turned the light back on, and snatched the small white envelope marking her place out of the book, opened it and laughed out loud. "Well, I'll be my great Aunt Fanny. Hello Mr. Mantle!"

The day before the Fourth, Angela, Daisy and Rose were back at Sammy T's in Fredericksburg with Elyse Dove and her son. They had just spent an hour over lunch telling them the whole story of Abby and Brad Douglas. And what they knew of how Margaret died.

Then Rose said, "We have something for you. Mother found it wedged against the dresser in my room the night that Abby broke in and tried to kill me."

Angela said, "I just picked it up and stuck it in my book. Isn't that the craziest thing?" She opened a small gift bag and handed Elyse a frame which held the Mickey Mantle autographed card, ticket stub and scorecard.

Tears sprang into her eyes as she gently touched the glass. "I can't believe it. I never thought we'd see this again."

Carl Dove said, "Can we keep it? Don't they need it for the trial?"

Daisy said, "No. Luckily with the confession that we taped, Abby is doing the only practical thing. She's pleading guilty. There won't be a trial."

Elyse stood up holding the card close and said, "Thank you." Carl took her arm and they left the restaurant.

Daisy, Rose and Angela followed. Angela hugged each of them tightly and said, "Home, girls. It's time to go home."

ROSE'S COCKTAIL HOUR

PEARL HARBOR
The perfect little cocktail to get you bombed!

¾ ounce Vodka
¾ ounce Melon Liqueur
Pineapple juice

Pour into Collins glass half filled with ice. Fill with pineapple juice.
Garnish with Maraschino cherries, stems attached.

MAI TAI
When it's hot and your sister's being way too nosy, it's time for a very fancy drink

½ ounce spiced rum
½ ounce white rum
½ ounce crème de almond
½ ounce triple sec
2½ ounces orange juice
2½ ounces pineapple juice
Splash of lime juice

Mix and pour into Collins glass half filled with ice.
Garnish with fruit slices and a little umbrella.

MIDSUMMERNIGHT'S DREAM
A lovely pink concoction for the after-burglary debrief

5 fresh strawberries, crushed
1 tsp. strawberry liqueur

1 ounce cherry brandy
2 ounces vodka
Tonic

Put all ingredients into a shaker with ice. Shake well.
Pour into a tall glass and fill with tonic. Garnish with a
strawberry.

FIRE CRACKER
A little pick-me-up for when the dog house catches fire

Pour over five cubes of ice in an old-fashioned glass:
2 ounces dark rum
½ ounce Sloe gin
Fill with orange juice
Top with a splash of Bacardi 151 Rum
Garnish with orange slice.

FROZEN CONCOCTION
*Just the thing when the dog's been duct-taped and you've
been conked on the head*

6 oz. can of frozen limeade concentrate
6 oz. rum
3 oz. triple sec
12 oz. water
Ice cubes

Mix in blender until slushy. Serve in a tall glass with a
cherry.

DAIQUIRI
First date? A little nervous? Let Angela fix you right up

1 jigger light rum
1 oz. lime juice
1 tsp. confectioner's sugar

Shake ingredients with shaved ice, strain over ice in an old-fashioned glass, and garnish with lime slice.

GOOD OLD SUMMERTIME
The name says it all!

1½ oz. vodka
Juice of ⅛ lemon
¾ oz. Sweet and Sour Mix* (homemade or purchased)
3 oz. soda water
1 tsp. confectioner's sugar

Shake all ingredients with ice and strain into an ice-filled Collins glass. Garnish with orange slice, lime slice, and cherry.

*Sweet and Sour Mix –
   Bring to boil 1 cup water and 1 cup sugar, just until sugar is dissolved.
   Take off heat and add 1 cup lemon juice and 1 cup lime juice. Mix and refrigerate.

SANGRIA
It's been a long day and you're a little down. Cheer up with some wine-laced fruit

1 bottle of good white wine
½ cup Vodka
½ cup white grape juice
½ cup sliced grapes (seedless, green or red)

1 green apple, sliced
½ pineapple, sliced
2 cups ginger ale

Pour wine and vodka in the pitcher and add sliced grapes, tangerine and pineapple. Next add sugar and stir gently. Chill mixture for at least one hour. Add club soda just before serving. (If you'd like to serve your Sangria right away, use chilled white wine and club soda and serve over lots of ice).

MIDNIGHT MARAUDER
Planning a late night escapade? Before you set out, enjoy a little liquid courage

2 oz. Vodka
6 oz. orange juice
Splash of cream soda

Serve over ice in a tall glass. Garnish with a cherry.

HURRICANE
When the wind is howling and a psycho comes knocking, drink up!

1 oz. light rum
1 oz. dark rum
2 oz. passion-fruit juice
1 oz. orange juice
½ oz. grenadine syrup
A squeeze of lime

Shake, strain into hurricane glass full of ice. Top with a squeeze of fresh lime juice and serve with straw.

NAKED RUNNER
The perfect evening – Pictionary, good friends, and gin!

Splash of ginger ale
2 oz. gin
2 oz. coconut rum
2 oz. cranberry juice
2 oz. pineapple juice

Serve in a tall glass over ice. Garnish with melon balls.

Author Bio

Penny Clover Petersen began writing her first novel at fifty-nine on a dare from her husband, Tom. A life-long resident of the Washington DC area, they now reside in Bowie Maryland.

In addition to writing, she enjoys spending time with her family, refurbishing old furniture, collecting stories for the 'family cookbook', and savoring new cocktail recipes.

She loves historic homes and is a docent at Riversdale Mansion in Riverdale, MD. Penny is currently at work on her third Daisy & Rose mystery.